About the author

John Taylor was brought up in Southall in Middlesex and left
school at sixteen to work in a series of short term jobs which
included office clerk, illustrator, hospital porter, builder's
labourer, milkman and mortuary attendant. He later studied
Drama and Education at the New College of Speech and
Drama and worked as an actor and writer in Theatre-in-
Education. He was a resident writer at Nottingham Playhouse, and for six months stage manager at the Khan Theatre
in Jerusalem. He taught in London for several years and took a
MA in the Philosophy of Education at the University of
London. Since 1986 he has been a producer for BBC Radio, a
job he now does part time in order to leave space for writing
and for family life. He lives in Greenwich in London with his
wife and daughter.

The UNOPENED CASEBOOK

of SHERLOCK HOLMES

Six Extraordinary Adventures

JOHN TAYLOR

BBC BOOKS

For Teresa

Published by BBC Books,
a division of BBC Enterprises Limited,
Woodlands, 80 Wood Lane, London W12 0TT

First Published in 1993

© John Taylor 1993

ISBN 0 563 36472 6

Typeset by Phoenix Photosetting, Chatham, Kent
Printed and bound in Great Britain by Clays Ltd, St Ives Plc
Cover printed by Clays Ltd, St Ives Plc

CONTENTS

FOREWORD

There exists in the human psyche a powerful tendency to mistake the obscure for the marvellous, and to construe as miraculous or diabolical that which is merely unexplained. We are all too eager to grasp at mystical solutions to even the most ordinary problems. Most of us will be familiar with those moments of dazed bewilderment experienced, for example, when a fountain pen is mislaid, or an umbrella discovered in a place other than the one in which we thought we had left it, when we find ourselves forming ludicrous hypotheses about haunted rooms or household imps.

Those of you familiar with the investigative methods of my friend and colleague, Sherlock Holmes, will be aware of the relentless campaign he waged against such a pitiable acquiescence of rationality in the face of the unknown, and this collection of stories, hitherto unpublished, celebrates precisely that aspect of his life's work.

I have chosen to leave out a number of intriguing tales which might be thought at first glance to merit inclusion. Some, like the chilling story of *The Cockroach Emporium*, have the right occult ingredients, but depend for their solutions as much upon luck as upon the power of systematic reasoning. Others, like the case of *The Village Vanishings* and the tragic adventure of *The Screaming Tower* are omitted because, while they demonstrate the flawless logic of Holmes' methods, their references to persons of innocent involvement make them currently unsuitable for publication.

There remain, however, these six singularly fascinating mysteries, each of which confronts the mind with just that sort of question likely to tempt it into supernatural speculation. How can an organ play in a locked church, a corpse go walking from its tomb, a woman disppear from a train in a mountain tunnel? Are there yet witches in Paddington, giant worms in Battersea and unnameable horrors in Charlton? Holmes never embarked upon any case, of course, with the presumption that a supernatural explanation was impossible. His business, as he saw it, was rather to discover whether it was the *most* rational interpretation of the facts and, if not, what better one could be found to replace it.

These stories demonstrate, I believe, not only the immense intellectual vigour with which he undertook these tasks, but also the irresistible passion which fuelled his search, a search for nothing less than the truth. I offer this small collection as a tribute to his peculiar genius.

John H Watson MD

= 1 =

THE WANDERING CORPSE

The adventure I am about to chronicle occurred during the first period in which Holmes and I shared lodgings in Baker Street at the time when my friend's reputation was beginning to spread. Our suite of rooms was comfortable, consisting of a bedroom apiece and a large, communal sitting-room. We got along pretty well, eating together, smoking together, spending a certain amount of time in idle talk and a good deal more in companionable silence.

On the evening upon which the extraordinary Smallbone affair began, we sat in the comfortable chairs either side of a blazing fire. I was restless. My old leg injury had decided to remind me of its existence and I could no longer concentrate on the book I was reading. I rather wanted to talk but Holmes, engrossed in a magazine article, appeared oblivious to my presence. Then, quite suddenly, he put the magazine down on his lap, looked me in the eye and said, 'Watson, I should appreciate your professional opinion.'

'Oh! Do you mean that you are sick, Holmes?'

'No, no, my friend. I should appreciate your professional opinion of this . . .'

With a sudden flick of the hand, he sent the magazine hurtling across the fireplace into my lap. It was the *Journal of Experimental Medicine*, a publication with which I was slightly familiar from my days as a medical student.

'It's a well-respected journal,' I said, 'Why do you ask?'

'On page eighty-three, you will find an article by someone called Professor Smallbone. Do you know the fellow?'

'I cannot say I do.'

'Well, if what the man says in his article is true, you will know him soon enough, for he appears to be on the brink of what can only be described as a staggering advance in medical science.'

Turning to the article at once, I came upon a drawing depicting a man strapped to an operating table with what appeared to be wires leading from his head and chest into a sinister, barrel-shaped contraption. The caption beneath the picture said, 'Professor Einthoven's experimental galvanometer utilizes electricity to measure contractions of the heart.'

'This is not entirely new,' I said to Holmes, 'Einthoven's experiments have long been the subject of rumour.'

'I am not referring to Professor Einthoven, Doctor. Read on, please.'

And then I came to it. As I read through the ensuing columns I felt an overwhelming awe. The author of the article, Professor Smallbone, had been experimenting with electricity on the bodies of dead fish and small animals. The key paragraph read as follows:

> '. . . *after numerous attempts, each time adjusting the amount of the electrical charge to the nerve-cells, we succeeded in reviving to consciousness several fresh-water trout which had been out of water* for more than two hours. *We went on to achieve an equivalent success with a number of mammals, namely a shrew, a mouse and a rat,* each of which had been thirty minutes in a vacuum jar deprived of oxygen. *After revival, these animals resumed their normal way of life. It would not be going too far to say that medicine has taken the first, faltering steps in the godlike task of resuscitating the dead.*'

'Well my friend, what do you make of it?' Holmes had filled a pipe and was now engaged in trying to light it.

'Absolutely remarkable,' I said. 'I mean, if it is true. But the man is an eminent scientist. It must be true, I suppose. It is all rather disturbing, in a way.'

There was, however, no chance for further debate upon the matter. At that moment a knock on the sittingroom door signalled the arrival of Mrs Hudson, our housekeeper.

'For you, Doctor.' Mrs Hudson crossed the room and put a neat, blue envelope into my hand. 'The coffee won't be long, gentlemen. It's just brewing now.'

The letter had been sent to my previous lodgings and re-addressed to reach me at Baker Street. This puzzled me, for I was sure that most of my regular friends and clients had been informed that I was now sharing rooms with Holmes. I opened the letter at once. 'Good Lord,' I heard myself saying, 'Good gracious! Holmes, this is quite amazing.'

'My dear fellow, what is it?'

'Such an extraordinary coincidence. This letter comes from the residence of none other than Professor Horace Smallbone – the very man who wrote the article in this journal – the electrical man.'

Holmes, never greatly impressed by coincidences, nodded impatiently. 'Well what does it say, Doctor? What does it say?'

Here is the letter which I then read to Holmes:

'Dear Doctor Watson,

Though we have not had the pleasure of meeting one another, I am of course aware of your reputation both as a physician and as a man of honour and integrity. It is in desperation that I now throw myself upon these qualities in the hope that you will be willing to assist me with a most distressing matter. I can say no more in this letter, but you would incur my eternal respect and gratitude if you were able to attend at the above address immediately. Please do not show this to another soul. I am indebtedly

Yours,
Professor Horace S. Smallbone.'

'The ridiculous thing,' I said to Holmes, 'is that I have never so much as met the fellow, yet here he is asking me to go out to Hackney at half past eight in the evening on some clandestine errand.'

I was, indeed, torn between irritation and curiosity. I had no wish to go out, yet I dearly wanted to know what the business was about, especially since the Professor seemed to have received such a good opinion of me. 'At any rate,' I said eventually, 'I suppose I had better see what the man wants.'

'The woman, I think you mean,' said Holmes.

'Woman?'

'I believe you will find, Watson, that the author of that letter is of the female sex.'

'Why, Holmes, you haven't so much as seen the drift of the writing. There are occasions when I do believe you make these abstruse suggestions out of a kind of mischief. I'm sorry, but I must go and find a cab.' And I strode towards the door.

Holmes, however, was determined to have his parting shot. 'I think you will find her quite young and agreeable,' he said, 'but extremely clever. Enjoy your evening, Doctor.'

Professor Smallbone's house was situated in one of the leafy streets leading from Victoria Park. The area I found generally pleasant, but the house itself large and gloomy. Ivy had been allowed to run rampant, suffocating the brickwork and obscuring the windows. In addition, the house was separated from its iron gates by a narrow avenue of spruce and pine, creating an overall effect of ghostly melancholy.

The door was opened by a very pretty woman of about thirty, black-haired, expensively dressed, whom I guessed at once to be the mistress of the house. It seemed strange, particularly on such a dark night, that she should be admitting callers herself, but detecting in her eyes the presence of fresh tears, I recalled that I was doubtless walking into a most delicate situation.

'Doctor Watson?'

'I am he. Mrs Smallbone?'

'Come in, Doctor, please.'

It was clear at once that the woman was distressed. Her

movements were brisk and nervous and she could hardly bear to look me in the eye. Leading me into a brightly lit parlour where she showed me to a chair, she offered me a glass of brandy. While she poured it I looked around the room, a somewhat ornate but otherwise quite ordinary parlour, distinguished only by a number of rather well-executed family portraits hung around the walls, four on one side of the fireplace, two on the other. Light patches on the wallpaper from where two other pictures had apparently been taken down explained this failure of symmetry. As I was meditating upon these trivial matters, Mrs Smallbone suddenly caught my attention and began to speak rapidly.

'Doctor Watson, I apologize for these mysterious circumstances – the letter – bringing you here. There are good reasons for all of it. Do not think too badly of me, Doctor, but I'm afraid I have deceived you. The letter was not from my husband but from myself. My husband isn't here. I mean – he *is* here but I fear he won't be able to – oh heavens!'

And with that she sank down upon a lounge and began to sob. For want of a better remedy, I poured her a small draught of brandy.

'My dear young woman, you are quite distraught.'

'Oh Doctor Watson, you must help me. The most dreadful thing has happened.'

'Of course I will help if I can,' I said, sitting beside her. 'Here now.'

She did not take the glass from me but, instead, cupped her hands around mine in order to sip from it.

'Thank you, Doctor. Horace always spoke of you as the kindest of men.'

'Your husband spoke of me? But Professor Smallbone and I have never met.'

'Nevertheless, he knew you. I believe he was some years junior to you when you were studying medicine.'

I could not recollect having heard the name of Smallbone during my Edinburgh years, but in student life it is generally those above one in seniority by whose fame or infamy one tends to be impressed.

'When your name appeared once in a medical journal,' she continued, 'Horace said – oh, with such affection, "Doctor John Watson. There's a man to go to if you're ever in a fix." Well I am in a fix. In the most terrible fix. So I *have* come to you. Please prepare yourself for a shock, Doctor, and promise you will not jump to conclusions.'

I assured her that I would try to keep an open mind.

'Follow me,' she said. 'This way, if you will.'

She led me through the house by way of a long passage until we stopped at a wooden door. She took a key from a pocket in her dress, unlocked the door, and passed through it into darkness.

'Mind the staircase,' she warned. 'There will be light in a moment.'

It was a wooden staircase and it rocked palpably under our conjoined weights. I held fast to the balustrade on my right while hugging the wall to the left, of which the brickwork was cold. Mrs Smallbone stepped lightly and confidently down the steps ahead of me, as if almost eager to show me what was below in the cellar.

'Is it a long way down?' I asked, partly to maintain contact with my guide in the darkness.

'It is a deep cellar, Doctor. It was dug deep to accommodate the laboratory. Down here is where my husband worked.'

At the foot of the stairs her key dealt with a second door, but we had descended so far into the gloom that even the wink of light from the opening at the head of the staircase did not enable me to see her any longer, though I could hear a scraping sound as she pushed open the lower door. At that moment, suddenly, out of the darkness of that cellar, came screeches and whistles and gibberings so frantic and pitiful that they sounded to me for a moment like the wails of the damned.

'They will quieten down in a moment,' said Mrs Smallbone. 'We have surprised them.'

Then I became aware of a deep, persistent drone, like nothing I had heard before. Mrs Smallbone seemed to sense my apprehension.

'Don't be alarmed, Doctor. What you hear is an electrical

generator. Electricity was my husband's passion and everything down here is operated by it. Including the lights.'

She gave a turn to some contraption attached to the wall and, magically, light appeared from lanterns at various points in the cellar.

'They are incandescent filament lamps,' she said. 'Mr Joseph Swan, the inventor, was an acquaintance of my husband's. Soon the whole world will be lit by such devices.'

But I hardly heard her, for my eyes were now adjusting to the cellar and its contents. The first things I noticed were the cages lining one long wall and containing all manner of rare creatures. There were monkeys, a sloth, chickens, many rats and mice, a couple of African birds with dazzling plumage and a thin, dark-looking, green-eyed beast lurking in the corner of one of the hutches, which I took to be a feral cat, or perhaps even a small wildcat. This bizarre menagerie had become almost silent when Mrs Smallbone turned up the electric lamps. The only remaining protests came from a thin black monkey, madly rattling the chicken-wire front of his small prison. But it was a more familiar object in the centre of the cellar which drew my attention next, some sort of bed, or, at any rate, something in the shape of a bed, though quite bare. I was reminded of the picture of Einthoven's galvanometer which Holmes had showed me earlier that evening in the *Journal of Experimental Medicine*.

'This is where my husband did all his work,' said Mrs Smallbone, wearily, 'and there he is, Doctor.'

My eyes followed her pointing finger to a place in a shadowy corner of the cellar next to the electrical bed. There was certainly something there, something in a heap.

'Good Lord, is he ...?'

'He's dead, Doctor Watson. Horace is dead.'

Stooping to inspect the thing in the shadows, I found it to be, indeed, the body of a man, slumped against the wall, jacket and shirt open. Even if I had come two hours earlier, I could have done nothing for him, for he was as cold as a fish on a slab.

'Has he lain here long?' I asked.

'Since mid-afternoon. Oh I'd known it was coming. He's had a heart condition for years. All the strain he put himself under working on –' she gestured broadly, despairingly, 'all this. He was a great man, Doctor Watson. His experiments in resuscitation went far beyond anything medicine had hitherto imagined possible.' She looked at me with tears welling up in her large, dark eyes. 'But who will bring *him* back?'

I mumbled the few words of comfort I could find, but my blandishments sounded hollow in my ears. She put her hand on my arm. 'Is it possible we can get him upstairs and into a bed, Doctor Watson?'

'Yes, Mrs Smallbone,' I replied, 'that is the first thing we shall do.'

Though not a tall man, Professor Smallbone proved solidly built. It took me a full twenty minutes to haul him out of the cellar, through the house and up the main stairs to a bedroom. Eventually I sat panting in a chair while Mrs Smallbone undressed the corpse on the bed and covered it with a sheet.

'There, now he is at rest,' she said quietly. 'It was terrible to have him lying down there in that ghastly laboratory, yet I could not have moved him without your help. Thank you, Doctor. Horace was right. You are very kind.'

'But I should like to ask you, Mrs Smallbone,' I said, 'what made you send for *me*? I mean, anyone might have moved the body. One of the servants . . .'

'We have no servants, Doctor.'

This seemed extraordinary, for the house was a large one, and well-kept. 'None?'

'Oh, I have a day-maid who comes in to clean. But no one is prepared to live here. Can you blame them? The noise down there, the animals. But mostly my husband's experiments. Reviving those thought to be dead, Doctor Watson, is an idea which frightens people. You can imagine the sort of stories that circulate the neighbourhood concerning this house. Headless women walking the stairs; creatures who are half-man, half-baboon lurking in the gardens at night. All nonsense, of course. Those who are unable to understand science paint everything in the colours of their own superstitions and mistake progress for magic. Once word got around, no employee would dare to stay here.'

Then Mrs Smallbone sat in a chair on the opposite side of the room, speaking to me across the body on the bed. 'But you're right, of course. I didn't call you here just to carry Horace up out of the cellar. I intend to prevail upon your kindness for one more thing.'

'Which is?'

'I want you to examine my husband's body and, provided you are satisfied that heart failure was the cause of death, to write a death certificate to that effect, so that he can be decently buried.

'My husband's experiments were very expensive. Doctor Watson. All that equipment. He owed money – a lot of it – and there might be speculation that he took his own life to escape his debts. Save me from that scandal, Doctor. That is what I ask.'

'Do you not have a physician of your own to whom you could entrust the task?'

'To be honest, Doctor Watson, Horace acquired many enemies. His genius made lesser men feel jealous. There were those in the medical profession eager to brand him as at best a fool, at worst a cheat and a fraud.'

'Then I will do what you ask, Mrs Smallbone,' I said.

'Doctor,' she replied, 'I should be eternally grateful.'

My examination of the body confirmed what Mrs Smallbone had led me to expect, and what my own cursory observations had suggested, namely that the professor had died of a heart attack. Such deaths are more common among youngish men than is generally imagined, particularly, it seems, those of a passionate or obsessive nature. One sign of that obsessiveness appeared upon the gold wedding ring which now clung very tightly to the deceased professor's puffed-up finger. Engraved there were the name *Clarissa* and the legend *Love Beyond Death*. Full of pity for the young woman, I completed the examination as quickly as I could, made out a death certificate and took my leave.

Within two days the body of Dr Horace Smallbone was

interred in the Smallbone family vault in Stoke Newington Cemetery. I could not refuse Clarissa Smallbone's request that I attend. There were, she said, few who had been kind enough to her husband during his life to be welcome now at his funeral. She arrived alone, except for her own elderly parents and a grim looking man who turned out to be a distant cousin of the deceased.

After the body had been laid to rest, Clarissa insisted that we return to the Smallbone residence in Hackney, where we drank tea, ate dainty sandwiches and made small talk until the grim cousin declared that he must return to Acton and his duties as Vaccination Officer. Having said my farewells to Clarissa, I shared a cab with him as far as Baker Street, during which journey he told me that he believed Professor Horace Smallbone to have been a man insane to the point of menace and that, blood relation or not, it was no small relief to him that his cousin had departed this life. I replied that many men of genius had been deemed insane before the world felt the full impact of their discoveries. To this he merely harrumphed and we spent the remainder of the trip in silence.

It was two days later than I received the remarkable letter whose contents were to make this case such a *cause célèbre*. It came late in the morning and proved to be from a much-respected colleague, one Edward Davey, a descendant of the esteemed chemist Sir Humphrey Davey and a scientist of some note himself.

Holmes and I were at breakfast, he with his nose in the morning papers, as I opened the envelope: but before I had finished reading, I had let out such a litany of gasps and exclamations as to excite my poor friend to a positive fever of curiosity. 'Watson,' he said impatiently, 'my dear chap, for heaven's sake either refrain from making those noises or have the goodness to tell me what is in that confounded letter.'

This is what I read him.

My Dear John

It is indeed a most bizarre situation that prompts me to put pen to paper, and I hope you will not misconceive my reasons for writing to you. I do so in order to put you on your guard against invidious gossip.

I spent this morning sitting in Hyde Park reading The Times, *where the obituary column informed me of the death of a certain Professor Horace Smallbone, from a heart attack at his Hackney home. Your name was mentioned as having attended the funeral.*

When I had finished reading, I folded the newspaper and walked from the park to purchase some small item at Butler's Pharmacy, which is situated in a passageway in Knightsbridge. There I encountered an astounding phenomenon.

Six feet from me a man was buying shaving soap, a razor and other items. John (I am quite sure of this, for I had met him professionally on a number of occasions) that man was none other than Professor Horace Smallbone himself, as large as life. I am fairly sure, however, that he did not see me.

My dear friend, I know not what deception is being practised, but implore you for the sake of your reputation not to become besmirched by any chicanery. I await your call, should you think me able to assist in any way, and remain, as ever,

> *Your loyal friend*
> *Edward Davey'*

I had, of course, familiarized Holmes with the details of the Smallbone business – the laboratory, the corpse and everything and he had received these facts with his usual coolness. I believe, however, that he was as shocked as I by the contents of Davey's letter, though his temperament enabled him to conceal it better.

'Extraordinary,' he said.

'Indeed. If Davey is correct.'

'Is he likely to be mistaken? Or to deceive?'

'Good Lord, no. He is as honest as the day is long. Yet, Holmes, Smallbone is dead! I saw his mortal remains laid to rest in the family vaults. For goodness' sake, the dead don't walk!'

He handed the letter back to me. 'I have heard that a man's hair may continue to grow after his death,' said he. 'But, I am certain, this must be the first recorded instance of a corpse popping out to purchase a razor.' He paced the room for a few moments before spinning around to face me.

'Watson – in which cemetery was the man interred?'

'In Stoke Newington. But Holmes, we have no authority to go about opening burial vaults.'

'Never mind the authority. Before we send for a cab, answer me one question. Apart from the electrical paraphernalia and the basement menagerie, was there anything about Professor Smallbone's house that struck you as odd?'

'I don't think so. It is an ordinary house. A little gloomy for my own taste. I don't recall nothing anything else. Oh one thing, but so trivial that –'

'Tell me, Watson. Trivial things can be pertinent.'

'Well there were two square patches on the sittingroom wall. Clearly some pictures had been taken down quite recently. That is all.'

Inexplicably, this seemed to excite Holmes immensely. 'Take heart, my friend, there is no puzzle which does not have its solution. Now let us get a cab and go and investigate that tomb.'

We did not go directly to the cemetery. Holmes was too methodical to rush around wasting time and effort where a little influence would cut corners. It happened that Mr Jeremiah Ballantyne, one of the governors of Stoke Newington cemetery, had once had occasion to consult Holmes about some thefts from a tomb, and that Holmes had cleared the matter up so briskly that he had declined to accept a fee. Cashing in upon this debt of gratitude, my colleague directed the cabbie to deliver us to Mr Ballantyne's office, where he promptly requested the loan of the master key to the Smallbone family vault. The request was not greeted happily for, as

Ballantyne put it, entering a man's tomb is hardly less audacious than barging into his bedroom while he is asleep, but
after Holmes had spun him some yarn about needing to protect Clarissa Smallbone from a possible scandal, he was persuaded that the only gentlemanly thing to do was to yield up
the key at once.

From Ballantyne's offices our cab took us on the short journey to Stoke Newington cemetery where we quickly located
the grave and descended the narrow stone steps to the locked
door of the Smallbone family vault.

Holmes opened the creaking door into the chill darkness.
For a moment I recalled the instant a few days before when
Clarissa Smallbone had led me into the cellar beneath her
house. It struck me as poignant that her husband, having
spent his working life in one damp subterranean vault, should
be now permanently interred in another, as though something
in him could not tolerate the natural light of day. The thud of
the door closing woke me out of my reverie.

'Holmes – must we shut ourselves in? The air in here is not
pleasant and I cannot see a thing.'

'I'm afraid I must lock it. It was, you'll remember, a condition of our borrowing this key that no one should see us here.
You heard what Ballantyne said: "A most inordinate request."'

Holmes locked the door and, lighting a match, applied it to
the dark-lantern he had brought with him. 'There. Now we can
see a little.'

Getting no response from me, he held the lantern to my
face, where he must have encountered an expression of some
misery and reluctance, for he said, 'Come, Watson. You are a
physician. Surely the dead hold no terrors for you?'

'Now see here, Holmes,' I replied, 'I am perfectly at ease in
the company of a good honest corpse that will lie down and
stay down. It is the walking variety I am not accustomed to.'

My friend laughed genially. 'Well, let us see if the wanderer
has returned. I take it this is the coffin?'

In contrast to the others in the vault which were earthy and
cobwebbed, the one I had watched the undertakers lay on the
slab a few days before bore hardly a speck of dust.

'Hold the light, my friend.'

He passed me the dark-lantern and began to lever his fingertips under the coffin-lid, which had neither screws nor nails in it. It seemed to me like the worst kind of sacrilege to be thus invading a man's final resting place, and my friend sensed my discomfort.

'Come, come. We wish the fellow no evil. Our purpose is quite legitimate. Help me lift it clear.'

Removing the lid, we laid it to one side. Then Holmes retrieved the lantern and shone it into the coffin. It was quite empty.

'Good Lord, Holmes!'

'Yes,' said he, 'I was not expecting this.' His coolness irked me and I said irascibly, 'But don't you see – it *must* have been Smallbone that Davey saw in Knightsbridge!'

He began to sniff the air of the coffin in large draughts. 'Can you smell it, Watson?' He put his finger into the box, felt about, and withdrew it again. 'Soap,' he said, 'Honeysuckle soap, Your olfactory memory might tell you that you had encountered it before.'

'My olfactory . . . ?'

'Your memory for smells. Think, my friend.'

At that instant, however, a terrible sound made both Holmes and myself jump with surprise. Footsteps were descending the stone steps outside the vault.

Holmes gestured to me to help him replace the lid on the coffin, an operation we expedited in frantic haste, then he held the lantern high and shone it around the tiny vault, pointing to the tressle upon which another of the coffins was standing.

'Hide behind there,' he whispered, and I obeyed instantly while he, extinguishing the lantern, slipped away into the shadows. A key had turned in the vault door and, as it began to open, daylight poured in and the pretty and delicate figure of Clarissa Smallbone appeared in the doorway.

It seemed to me that she entered that cold place with some trepidation, stopping just inside the open door to take stock. She sniffed the air, and I wondered whether she had detected

14

the odour of lamp-oil in the vault. She took from her shoulder a large carpet-bag, removing from it some objects which I could not quite make out. Then, approaching the empty coffin, she employed one of these items as a tool to lever up the lid and, with difficulty, but systematically, released it and slid it away from the box. It occurred to me that without a lantern she could probably not actually see into the coffin. But when she put an arm into it, she froze in horror. She felt about frantically inside, then screeched one word 'Horace!' and fainted dead away.

We carried her quickly into the sunshine, but before I was able to revive her, Holmes said to me with great intensity, 'Watson, we say nothing to her about our having been hiding in that vault. It is essential.' So a little afterwards, when Clarissa Smallbone opened her eyes and looked at me in utter, helpless confusion, I said, 'It's all right, you are in Stoke Newington cemetery. It is Doctor Watson. And this is my friend Mr Holmes. We heard you cry out your husband's name and ran to find you unconscious in the tomb.'

'He's gone!' she said.

'Yes,' I said, 'we noted that the coffin was empty.'

'But what is it? What's going on?'

'We do not know,' I said. 'It is a mystery. But we will do our best to help sort it out, I promise.'

'Doctor,' she said, 'take me home, please. I am so frightened.'

After escorting Clarissa to her home, where the day-maid agreed to put her to bed and look after her, Holmes and I took a cab back to Baker Street. The peculiarity of the business stimulated me to speculate noisily as we journeyed home, but it had reduced Holmes to one of his profound, cogitative silences. In the end, I acquiesced, and we spoke no more about the matter until, that evening, after supper, Holmes lit a pipe and said, 'Well, Watson, what do you make of it all?'

'What do I make of it? I believe,' I said, for I had been giving

the matter some thought, 'that there is only one possible conclusion. Professor Smallbone had been engaged upon experiments whose aim was to resuscitate unconscious bodies
with electricity. That method has now been used upon him.'

'You say resuscitate "unconscious" bodies, Doctor. Yet you
certified him dead. Was he not dead?'

'Well, yes. By all normal signs and tests.'

'As dead as a Christmas goose is how you put it to me last
evening.'

'Yes I did. I was quite certain at the time.'

'Then why be shaken from your certainty now?'

'Because the fellow's coffin is empty. Because he was seen
strutting about in Knightsbridge.'

'The line of least resistance, Watson. How many times must
I say it? Which is most likely, that a man has been resurrected
from the dead or that we have overlooked an alternative
explanation?'

'The latter,' said I, 'and I was quite sure that there must be
such an explanation, with Clarissa somehow implicated. But
when we observed her in the vault and she saw that her husband was missing from that coffin, I am quite certain that her
reaction was one of genuine shock. You heard her shriek his
name.'

'I agree that her surprise was genuine,' said my friend, 'and
that is, indeed, a point of great interest. Nonetheless, we must
not be waylaid by the impossible while there are still mere
improbables to be investigated. Those items she took from
the carpet-bag. Did you look at them?'

'Why, no,' I said, 'I completely forgot about them.'

'Two sets of pliers,' he announced, 'the handles of one set
being the tool she employed to wedge open the coffin. But
why did she want to open it at all? What else, if anything, did
she mean to do with the pliers?

'I don't know,' I said. 'It is most strange.'

At this moment Mrs Hudson interrupted us to say that
someone was waiting below. 'For you, Mr Holmes, sir. A Mrs
Aubrey. I did say it was a bit late but she seems on the desperate side.'

'Show her up, Mrs Hudson, thank you. And bring us some coffee, if you would.'

Mrs Aubrey, it was clear, was not accustomed to the taste of coffee, for she grimaced at its bitterness and put the cup back in its saucer. She was perhaps thirty or thirty-five, pretty in a care-worn way, the very picture of genteel poverty. Her speech showed her to be an educated woman but her clothes, though clean and neat, were neither new nor fashionable. Yet she was graceful and of strong character and answered Holmes's questions directly and honestly.

'You have come far, Mrs Aubrey?'

'It's a good step from Holborn, Mr Holmes.'

'You walked then?'

'Yes, I walked. And I'd better tell you now, I've little money. If that disqualifies me from entitlement to your services, I'd be glad if you'd say so.'

'Let's talk about your problem, Mrs Aubrey. I'm sure it will be more interesting than talking about money.'

'Thank you. That's very good of you.'

Momentarily, she hesitated. Then, taking her courage in both hands, she began her story.

'It's my husband Albert I've come about. The difficulty is . . . well, the difficulty is that he has earned himself something of a reputation. His work has been at best casual, and at worst, illegal. He has in the past been to prison, I'm afraid, and although I know him to be a changed man, the police do not, I think, believe in such reformations. He has twice been arrested on suspicion of crimes he had no connection with, purely on account of his history. Which is why, when he went missing, I could not go to them for help.

'Your husband is missing?'

'Since Saturday morning. He went off to his job, and never returned.'

'And where was the job?'

'This is what worries me. He'd been working for the scientist – Professor Smallbone.'

Holmes and I exchanged incredulous glances, but Mrs Aubrey, absorbed in her story, continued:

17

'I expect you know, Mr Holmes, that on Saturday night the professor died. And to be honest, sir, I'm worried. Albert is only a laboratory assistant, but he devotes himself to the work and felt he was worth more than he was paid. There'd been arguments about hours and pay and all sorts of other, more elusive things. Then just lately Albert said to me, "I can't tell you anything in detail, Hannah, because I have sworn an oath, but I know something about our Professor Horace Smallbone that would shake Hackney down to its golden boots."

'Mr Holmes, what worries me is this – why did Albert disappear directly after the Professor's death? My guess is that they had another argument, perhaps a fight, and that it precipitated the Professor's heart attack. In fear of what would happen to him, because of his past, Albert has run off somewhere. But whatever went on in that house on Saturday, Mr Holmes, I'm quite certain my husband is no murderer.'

Holmes replied to the woman quietly, 'Mrs Aubrey, you can rest assured, Professor Smallbone was not murdered. Your husband is innocent of any blame, I am certain.'

'Then where is he? Why hasn't he come home? Do you think he is all right?'

Holmes spoke gravely. 'I cannot give you any definite answers at the moment. I want you to leave your address with my housekeeper, Mrs Hudson, who will arrange for a cab to take you home, and I will be in touch with you directly I have finalised this matter, which I expect to be first thing tomorrow morning.'

Holmes sent for our housekeeper and, full of gratitude, if still somewhat troubled, Mrs Aubrey went, leaving us to watch her departing cab from the sittingroom window.

'Watson,' said Holmes, 'we must go out.'

'Now? But where?'

'Back to the Smallbone's house at Hackney. The last piece of our puzzle has just turned up.'

In the cab Holmes told me his plan. I was to be dropped at the Smallbone residence in Hackney and to delay whomever I found there with idle chatter until he returned. As the cab stopped at the end of the Smallbone's driveway, Holmes warned me solemnly to be careful, and promised to get back as soon as he possibly could. As his cab disappeared, I walked up the drive and knocked on the door of the house.

The Clarissa Smallbone that answered the door was a very different woman from the gentle and vulnerable creature who had welcomed me on that first evening of our acquaintanceship. As she recognized me, her eyes seemed to turn to little spheres of ice.

'Doctor Watson – John, it is very late.'

'It is,' I replied, 'but I have ...' (I found myself fumbling for an excuse to stay) 'I have some information. That is to say – there are one or two things which ... May I come in for a moment, Clarissa?'

With some reluctance, she showed me into the sittingroom. Since she had opened the door to me herself, I had imagined that the day-maid was gone home, yet I had a sense of someone else being present in the house.

'Are you alone?' I asked.

'Yes. I could not tolerate company today. Tomorrow I shall go to the police and tell them what has happened. It was bodysnatchers I suppose that took Horace from the coffin?'

It occurred to me that, from her point of view, this would be the natural explanation of the afternoon's events.

'Oh – yes, I dare say.'

'I was grateful for what you did this afternoon,' she continued, 'reviving me like that, and bringing me home.'

'It was the least we could do.'

'I had just come to pay Horace a visit. It was a terrible shock.'

'Of course. Terrible.'

Her tone changed a little. 'I must say, when I thought about it afterwards, I was at a loss to know what you were doing in Stoke Newington cemetery this afternoon with Mr Holmes.'

For this I was completely unprepared. 'Mr Ballantyne, one of the governors of the cemetery, had asked us to investigate some thefts,' I said hastily.

'In your role as detectives?'

19

'Well, yes.'

'I did not know, when I first asked you here, that you were a colleague of Sherlock Holmes.'

'It is not widely known.'

'He is, I imagine, an astute man. A marvellous brain, I dare say.'

'Oh, first class.'

'And I know he exhibits that inveterate curiosity which is the engine of so many great minds.'

'Oh,' said I, trying to brighten things up, 'I dare say his curiosity will get the better of him one day. But his heart's in the right place.'

She glowered at me as though I could not have made a more contemptuous statement. 'Oh is it? Oh well, I suppose if his heart's in the right place he can poke his celebrated aquiline nose wherever he likes.'

Her sudden attack knocked me off balance and I enquired whether she was upset.

'Upset? I am furious, Doctor Watson. I sent you that first pleading letter in the strictest confidence. I particularly asked you to tell no one about my husband's tragic death. Now this Sherlock Holmes of yours seems to be privy to everything. And *you* are hiding things from me.'

'But not for long,' said a man's voice behind me, and then, 'No. Don't turn round. I have a gun trained on you, Doctor.'

The voice was grim and cruel and it was seconds before I found my voice.

'Might I know who you are sir?'

'Never mind that, Doctor. You know the way to the cellar, I believe. Please make your way there now.'

Holmes' warning of the possibility of some kind of treachery had not prevented this sudden attack from quite unnerving me, and I trembled as I was made to follow Clarissa down into the cellar where I was instructed to lie down on the electric bed. Clarissa attached to my wrists circular pieces of copper, connected to wires leading from the machine. The man, whom I could only surmise to be Professor Smallbone himself, remained behind me, out of view.

'You are a medical man, Doctor Watson. You will know the expression, "electric shock". Well here is a machine which gives very large electric shocks indeed. Now, I want you to tell me everything you know about this business.'

'I know nothing,' I said, 'except that a body has disappeared from the Smallbone family vault in Stoke Newington cemetery.'

A bolt of indescribable pain shot along my arms and across my chest, knocking the breath out of me and causing me to shake uncontrollably.

'For pity's sake,' I cried, 'what are you doing?'

'Trying to get to the truth, Doctor,' said the man, not without some pleasure. 'Now, I'll ask you again what you know.'

'I know,' I said, 'that Professor Smallbone was seen after his death in a shop in Knightsbridge. I say Professor Smallbone. It may have been his double.'

'Is that what Mr Holmes thinks?'

'I've no idea what Holmes thinks. He does not always confide in me.'

'Come along, Doctor Watson,' said Clarissa, 'there's more.'

'No,' said I, 'there isn't.'

Another thunderclap of pain racked me, and so desperate was I for this not to be repeated that I searched my memory for anything else I could tell them.

'Well there is the question of the missing man,' I said, 'Albert Aubrey.'

The voice behind me was suddenly cold as steel. 'What do you know about him?'

I was about to reply that the man's wife had visited us, but fearing this could put the woman in danger, thought better of it.

'He's lost his tongue, Clarissa. Give him another dose.'

I braced myself for another bolt of pain, but it never came. Instead, a familiar voice shouted from the vicinity of the laboratory door, 'Sherlock Holmes here, Professor Smallbone. I can tell you all you need to know.'

Then my friend addressed me directly.

'Forgive me for leaving you alone in the hands of these

21

monsters, my friend. I had to clear one final thing up – and to let the police know of the intentions of these people to escape.'

'Ha!' exclaimed Clarissa, 'what nonsense. Where are these police?'

'Surrounding the house,' said Holmes. 'You are trapped, I'm afraid. Look over your shoulder, Watson, and you will see the face of your torturer.'

Since it now seemed that Holmes had control of the situation, I ventured a look. I could hardly have been more surprised by what I saw. The man holding the gun was tall and thin with heavy, dark eyebrows – nothing like the man whose death I had certified.

'This is Professor Smallbone?'

'Yes, Watson. The man whom you found dead in this laboratory was Albert Aubrey, the husband of that poor woman who came to visit us today. They murdered him – using the very machine to which you are now attached, which no doubt simulates very exactly the symptoms of a heart attack.'

'Why should a man like me kill a useless fool like Aubrey?' said Smallbone with contempt.

'Because, Professor, he knew that your experiments to revive the dead were a total failure. Even that magazine article was a fraud, and when Aubrey threatened to tell the world as much, you cold-bloodedly despatched him.

'The disposal of the corpse is the most irksome and dangerous of a murderer's tasks, but you hit upon the idea of using Aubrey's to your advantage. If it could be passed off as your own dead body, it could be disposed of in an ordinary grave, and you, as far as the world was concerned, would be deceased, thereby exempting you from your excessive debts. The final thing I had to clear up, Watson, was the matter of Professor Smallbone's assets. As I suspected, he has been transferring capital into the bank account of one Doctor John Isenk for some weeks. Doctor John Isenk was to be his alias after the Professor's supposed demise.' At this point he turned back to Smallbone. 'You needed a death certificate, of course, and for this purpose Doctor Watson here was summoned.

Then all you had to do was move to another part of the world. But, to ensure that Doctor Isenk was not immediately recognized as yourself, you decided to shave off your distinctive black beard. That was what took you to Butler's pharmacy in Knightsbridge, where you were spotted by a friend of Doctor Watson's, Mr Edward Davey.

'What Davey did not realize, however, was that you had seen him too. Alarmed that investigations of the tomb might be made, you went there yourself and removed the body of Albert Aubrey from the coffin. However, since you'd not had the chance to alert your wife to these plans, when she went to the tomb herself, she was genuinely horrified to find the coffin empty.'

'But she called out her husband's name,' said I.

'Yes,' said Holmes, 'and that confused me too at the time. Did that not mean that she thought it was her husband's body that was missing from the coffin? But then, what is more natural, when a woman is in shock, than that she should call on the name of her husband and accomplice?'

'But why,' said I, 'was she at the tomb at all, if not to visit a deceased husband?'

'You remember that you mentioned that the body you examined was wearing a tight-fitting ring. Clearly, Mrs Smallbone had put the ring upon the finger of the corpse prior to your arrival, so that you would believe it to be her husband's body. Well, with the finger swelling after death, and Aubrey being a bigger-built man than Professor Smallbone, she found she was unable to remove it. She had tried to use soap—hence that smell of honeysuckle and the trace of soap we found in the coffin—but had failed. On the day she interrupted us in the vault, she had returned for another attempt, this time with two pairs of pliers—one pair to hold the finger, the other to remove the ring.'

'But where is the corpse now?'

'In the vault, Watson. It was never anywhere else.'

'What?'

'The Professor here was working on his own. How far could he carry it? I am certain he only moved it out of one coffin, and into another, already occupied. You will find that the unfortunate Albert Aubrey is currently bedfellow to a more venerable Smallbone corpse.'

At this point, Smallbone himself broke in desperately. 'I am not going to let you arrest us, Holmes. If you force me, I'll kill you both.'

'I must warn you,' said Holmes boldly, 'that before I came down here I located the steam generator which powers this laboratory, and closed the regulator valve. A large head of steam will by now have built up and I feel we would all be safer above ground.'

Clarissa Smallbone's eyes blazed furiously. 'Shoot them, Horace, and let's be done. To hell with you, Sherlock Holmes!'

But she had hardly finished her sentence when there was the most colossal bang from somewhere above us. Down in the cellar, wires fizzed and sparked frighteningly. Something made of glass exploded behind me and I turned to see Smallbone, apparently wounded by a flying splinter, staunching a bloody gash near his eye.

'Quick!' shouted Clarissa, 'let's get out.'

The caged beasts were in uproar now and there was pandemonium. Clarissa Smallbone, seeing her husband blinded with blood and unable to find his way forward, abandoned him and ran to the staircase. He called piteously, 'Clarissa! Help!' but she ignored him and started up the steps. Then Smallbone, still half-blinded, raised his pistol and fired a single wild shot. Perhaps he intended it as a warning, or as a desperate statement. At any rate, his tiny wife cried out once and toppled over the wooden balustrade, dead, with a bullet through the neck.

Holmes ran to grab the gun from Smallbone's hand, but the professor had already turned its barrel towards his own forehead. There was another sharp bang, his head shattered, and he fell.

It was left to the police, to clear up the mess. Holmes and I returned to our lodgings, and although we were both weary, I was keen to know the route by which my friend had arrived at a solution to the case, and questioned him upon the matter.

'Tell me, at what point did you suspect that Smallbone might not have died?'

'There were a number of odd things, my friend. First, those patches on the wall where pictures had been removed. What would be the point of taking down just two pictures? They must have been portraits of Professor Smallbone himself, concealed in case you should compare them to the face on the body in the laboratory. Then that business of the shaving equipment. Edward Davey never mentioned in his letter to you that the man he saw in the Knightsbridge pharmacy had a long black beard. Why should he? Since he thought you had seen the man, he assumed you would know. But only a man who has a beard and wishes to remove it buys shaving materials all at once. A clean-shaven man already owns them, and merely tops up with the occasional item. The corpse in the cellar, therefore, and the man in the shop, were not the same man.'

'Excellent, Holmes,' I said disconsolately. 'You have pulled it off again, old chap.'

'But Watson, why so gloomy?'

'I have been duped, Holmes. Clarissa Smallbone used me ruthlessly. If she had known I was sharing lodgings with Sherlock Holmes, she would have picked on another physician to sign that death certificate for her. It was a fool she wanted, and she thought she had found one in me.'

'Watson,' said Holmes, 'you are not a fool. Clarissa Smallbone was a very clever woman and, what's sometimes just as dangerous, a very beautiful one.'

'Yes,' I said, 'it is a terrible waste. And no one will raise *her* from the dead.'

'Let us hope not, Watson,' said Holmes with a chuckle, 'for both our sakes.'

2

THE BATTERSEA WORM

I had known Caspar Holland since medical school. When I went off to serve my time as an army surgeon, he was already setting up in practice in Clapham, not far from his father's residence in nearby Battersea. Holland's father was the famous climber Angel Holland, an inveterate traveller who had scaled most of the world's best-known peaks and whom I had met once or twice while his son and I were fellow students.

I had not communicated with young Holland, however, for almost four years, when a letter arrived from him one summer morning. This was in 1885, when Holmes and I had been some good while at our Baker Street lodgings, in those days when we were still both bachelors.

Holmes being away in Dorset, I had the rooms to myself for a few days, and when I came into the sittingroom to take a quiet breakfast I found that Mrs Hudson had left a letter propped up against the teapot. I knew at once from whom it came, for at university Holland and myself had so regularly traded notes and essays that his hand was almost as familiar to me as my own. Yet, despite the good memories of our friendship, I opened the letter with some trepidation, reflecting that contact with a lost acquaintance is as often renewed in tragic as in happy circumstances.

The news, however, seemed to be neither good nor bad, merely somewhat bizarre. The letter read as follows:

My Dear Watson,
What a pity that we have not seen one another for so
long. The world is a busy place and I think you and I
have been swept up thoroughly in the madness of it,
probably with some relish!

To get to the point, I am writing to you to ask a
rather substantial favour, which you must feel free to
refuse if it is inconvenient for you. All I can tell you for
the time being is that it would require five days of your
time and that the business concerns my father, with
whom I have been lodging at the family home for the
past two years. He would insist upon rewarding you
financially to a degree which I am certain you would
find generous. If you think you might be able to spare
that amount of time, come to Barrowfields on Friday
early. Otherwise, let me know. All will be revealed if, as
I hope, we meet.

Until which time I remain, as always, your
affectionate friend,

Caspar Holland M.D.

In such decisions the part played by curiosity cannot be underestimated. I had no great desire to leave Baker Street for five days for I had plenty to do of my own, yet I longed to know into what strange mission I was being pressed and, I confess, what magnitude of financial reward might be entailed in that voluptuous epithet 'generous'.

Holmes had not returned when Friday morning came, so I left him a note explaining that I should see him on the following Tuesday or Wednesday. I then packed an overnight bag and took a cab to Battersea.

It began to drizzle as we drove out of Oakley Street onto Albert Bridge. The river was littered with boats of all kinds, bobbing on brown, rain-pocked water. A little way on we turned right into the area just north of Clapham Junction where Barrowfields, the Holland family's large house, stands in its own grounds.

Caspar Holland welcomed me jovially and garrulously. We

were in Barrowfield's huge reception hall, out of which rose the great tower which made the house such a landmark, some would have said an eyesore, in the neighbourhood.

'Watson, my dear chap, what a joy to see you again. Was your journey good? You've not been here for years. There are changes, as you'll see. Here, let me take your hat. I dare say you could do with some tea. Or perhaps something stronger. Ah! I see you've spotted the Contraption.'

I had stopped dead in my tracks. Stretching from the floor right up into the tower was a slender, perpendicular construction of wrought iron. The top of it, barely visible, seemed to connect to a landing at the tower's summit. I had never seen anything like it.

'You might describe it,' said my host with glee, 'as a monument to Elisha Graves Otis. Except that I think the fellow is still alive.'

'Holland, what are you on about?'

'It is a passenger elevating machine. For short say elevator or passenger lift. Otis is the chap who invented it. An American. You'll notice that there are no stairs up to the gallery room. That is now is the only way up and the only way down.'

'I have read of such things,' I said, 'but never expected to find one in a traditional English home. There is a platform for the passengers?'

'Well, one steps into a sort of canister which is hauled up and down by steam. They are said to be working on an electrical version, but this is perfectly efficient. Later, you will travel in it.'

'If you so decree.'

'You'll love it, Watson. In the meantime, we'll have luncheon, and I'll explain everything.'

There were three servants at Barrowfields, Mrs Fowler the housekeeper who had taken a dislike to me from the moment she opened the front door, a young man called Jethro who fulfilled every function from coachman to bottle-washer, and a rather stout and amiable woman called Mrs Callendar who turned out to be not only very pleasant but also an excellent cook. The meal that was set before us was splendid. However, as Caspar Holland and I sat down to eat, it became apparent that his father was not to join us. I enquired what was the matter.

'He never comes down, Watson.'

'Comes down?'

'From that room in the tower. He has been there for two years.'

'But why?'

'Fear, Watson. Well, more like sheer terror. Odd, really. He was always such a hero to me. Still is in some ways. You should have seen him climb. Fearless. I've watched him beat an overhang above a thousand foot drop with nothing but his hands and feet, in a wind that froze your lips to your teeth.

'Then a couple of years ago he sent for me and pleaded with me to move back in with him. He could trust very few people, he said, but he hoped he could at least depend upon his own son. Since then he has never let me leave him in the house alone and, as a consequence, I have not had a holiday in two years. You know me, Watson, climbing is a passion for me too, and I'm not the sort who can hide his feelings easily. I became so miserable that in the end the old chap told me I must have some time away, on condition that I found a well established friend who was totally reliable – and preferably also a physician – to deputize as bodyguard in my absence. This narrowed the field, as you can imagine, but you were the perfect choice. He remembers you well and was delighted with my suggestion. As delighted, I mean, as he ever gets about anything.'

'I am flattered to be asked.'

'There's one more thing you need to know. A little after my arrival he heard of this American lift man, Otis, and put out an advertisement inviting competent engineers to tender for the contract to install such a device in the tower. The lift was erected and the staircase subsequently demolished. You see the point of it, I suppose?'

'Well, that nobody can sneak up unseen, I imagine.'

'Precisely.'

'But why does he fear for his life?'

'It's something he doesn't like talked about outside the

family. He will tell you himself in his own good time. At any rate, we shall go and see him directly we have finished luncheon.'

After the meal, we made our way back to the main hall. As we approached the passenger elevating machine we were greeted by the noise of a spanner clanking on metal. A swarthy man of about thirty years, in neat blue overalls, his mouth hidden by a black moustache, was tightening a nut near the door of the device.

'Ah! You're here, Cuthbert,' said Holland. 'Is everything in order?'

'I think so, Mr Holland.'

'Good. This gentleman is Doctor Watson. He'll be looking after things while I go on holiday.'

'Pleased to meet you, Doctor.'

'You'll be seeing quite a bit of Mr Cuthbert, Watson' said Holland. 'He comes in two or three times a week to maintain the elevator.'

'I am most impressed with it,' I said.

'Well, it's the tallest passenger elevator in the country, Doctor. Eighty-two foot from the bottom of the shaft to the top and safer than a perambulator. What's more, I check it every other day to make sure it stays safe. Which reminds me, Mr Holland, I'll need to look at the top of the shaft before I go.'

Something about the down-to-earth nature of the man inspired confidence, and I even found myself looking forward to my first trip in this extraordinary invention. While Cuthbert finished what he was doing, Holland pointed to a black rubber tube which ran up the outside of the perpendicular framework, culminating in a metal cup not unlike the speaking cone of a telephone.

'The lift can only be operated from the inside,' said Holland. 'It's Father's way of ensuring that no one can get up into the tower without his knowledge. *I* brought the elevator down this morning and until I return he can be certain he is alone up there. No one must ever travel up unless I am with them, or, from tomorrow, unless *you* are with them, Watson.'

He blew into the speaking tube. There was a distant whistle.

30

Holland continued to chatter to me while we waited for an answer. Then the tube squawked.

'Who is it?'

'Father, it's me. Doctor Watson has arrived from London'.

'Excellent. Bring him up at once.'

'Oh – and Mr Cuthbert needs to check the top of the lift shaft.'

'Very well.'

Holland replaced the tube on its hook. 'You must always let him know if anybody is going up or coming down with you,' he said solemnly.

I was to learn next what the component parts of Mr Otis's elevating invention were properly called. The perpendicular construction within which the lift rose and fell was known as the lift-shaft and the wrought-iron box in which the passengers travelled up and down that shaft was called the cage. We entered this by means of a wooden door, which was closed after us. Caspar Holland, Cuthbert the engineer and I could just squeeze into the small cube of space.

'Perhaps you'll show Doctor Watson how to drive it, Mr Cuthbert,' Holland said.

'Not much to it, Doctor,' said Cuthbert amiably, 'The engine is already pumping away. All you need do is throw this handle here that engages the cage with the gears.'

After a moment's hesitation I took the plunge and threw the lever. With a slight jerk we were off upwards. It was a most exhilarating sensation to see the floor, through the sides of the cage, receding rapidly. I had never before understood so keenly what it must be like to fly. The journey, for my liking, was over much too soon, as the cage locked itself against the upper platform and Holland opened the door.

'Marvellous,' I said, 'quite marvellous, Mr Cuthbert.'

Cuthbert thanked me and Holland said with a smile, 'You will have ample opportunity for more trips, Watson.'

While the engineer began to clamber upward to see to his machinery, Holland and I went to meet the old man. In fact, so much had he advanced in senility since our last meeting that, had I passed him on the street, I would not have known him.

'Decent of you to come,' said he.

'My pleasure, Mr Holland.'

'I shall call you John just as I did when you and Caspar were medical students. We'll have no false formalities.'

'As you please.'

'What do you think of my ivory tower?'

I looked about the room. It was almost circular, with windows looking in every direction, south toward Clapham with its vast lattice of railway lines, north towards the calm, brown river. Outside the window, running right around the tower, was a stone ledge, wide enough to obscure the view of the grounds below. Its function, I imagined, was to provide a platform for cleaning the windows. It could only be accessed by stepping out of one of the windows in the tower.

The room itself was sparsely but elegantly furnished. There were bookcases, a writing-desk, some antique cupboards and a large collection of magazines – everything necessary for a man of education and taste who considers himself to be under siege.

'It is very pleasant,' I replied.

'It is my home,' he said, with a trace of melancholy.

Holland rushed to prop up his father's flagging spirits.

'Let's have a drink and a cigar, Dad,' said he, opening the antique cupboard to reveal a *cache* of whisky. We drank and smoked for an hour, during which time I did my best to become reacquainted with Angel Holland. Certainly it was Caspar who did most of the talking, but this provided the opportunity to observe his father unobtrusively. I remembered him as a tall, thin man, very muscular, with that taut, wiry strength typical of many climbers which his son had inherited. When I first met him, Angel Holland had seemed to me not only physically powerful but morally and spiritually strong too. Now his bluntness, which I had then construed as the irascible spark of a fiery nature, had fizzled out into the petulance of tired old age.

When Mr Cuthbert knocked on the door to say that his inspection of the lift was complete, Holland and I took our leave of his father and escorted the engineer back to the ground floor.

'I'll need to come back to fit a new top wheel to the governor-cable. Ought to be sooner rather than later. Tomorrow suitable?'

'Well you must ask Doctor Watson,' said Holland with some pleasure, 'he is in charge for the next few days. I am off this afternoon.'

I said that Saturday would be perfectly convenient and Mr Cuthbert went on his way. Holland's excitement about his holiday was burgeoning as the minutes ticked on towards the departure time, and since excitement made him more and more talkative I was not a little relieved when, having visited his father one last time to make his farewells, he finally left the house at about five in the afternoon to catch a late train to Elder's Edge in Berkshire to be ready for his first climb on the very next morning.

Having wandered about the house for a while, I left Jethro the young coachman on sentry duty at the lift and went out to explore the garden. The rain had stopped but the evening was cloudy, shedding a yellowish light upon the mysterious old house. From the rear, the tower could be seen in its entirety, reaching too high beyond the rooftops to qualify for architectural elegance and, banded by the stone shelf under the windows, reminding me a little of a lighthouse and also, perhaps more forbiddingly, of the black peak of a mountain, unscalable in its sheerness.

I wondered about Angel Holland and what turn of events had converted so brave a man into such a timid one, imprisoning him in his tower-top nest for more than two years. Eventually curiosity got the better of me. I determined at last to ask him directly at the first opportunity.

Supper provided the perfect pretext. While Angel Holland ate, I remained in the tower with him, chatting about Caspar and his climbing holiday until I was able to steer the conversation towards Angel Holland's own distinguished career.

'You have had some remarkable adventures,' I said, 'Caspar used to regale me with them when we were students. But I never quite understood why you gave up climbing or why you chose to shut yourself away here.'

He stopped eating and stared at me. 'Caspar hasn't told you?'

'He said it was something you preferred strangers not to know about it.'

He seemed touched. 'God bless the boy. I did say that. Never expected he'd be able to keep it secret, though.' The thought seemed to mellow him. He put aside his plate.

'All right, John, you shall hear everything. Hope it won't make you think too badly of me. It's not a pleasant tale, that's for sure. You'd better pour us some whisky.'

I did as I was bade, and settled down to listen to Angel Holland's story.

'I have climbed in every corner of the globe but my last expedition was in Scotland, not far from Cairn Toul. There were four of us. McAndrew and Thorne had accompanied me on many climbs. They were brave, reliable, men of good sense and sound judgement. Not so Jack Laslett. Oh, no one could dispute his skills as a climber but he was intolerably self-opinionated and vain. Climbing must be a team project, not a competition between individuals. Laslett was a glory-hunter.

'The mountain we were tackling had no official name. We called it McAndrew's Fell after my companion, a man of local ancestry. This irked Laslett, who maintained that the name should have been decided by drawing lots, since no one of us had any greater right than any other to leave his mark upon the mountain. It was our first major argument and, after it, things never improved. Every decision the three of us made, Laslett contested. Sometimes we compromised, other times, for the sake of peace, we gave in to his demands. We reached the summit easily and with no injuries, but our fellowship had taken a thorough battering.

'As we began to descend, however, so did the weather. You know how fast it can change on the slopes. First the wind whipped up, then there was sleet, then snow. Visibility became dreadful. Suddenly it seemed as if our path down the mountain had been obliterated.

'Thorne, one of those fellows with a sense of direction as keen as a homing pigeon's, said he thought he could find the way down – but Laslett disputed his choice of route. We argued violently.

'The weather was worsening. Time was getting short for us. It would be dark soon and we had not made provision for an overnight camp. We voted to follow Thorne. Laslett dissented. He swore his own route was the correct one. He was shrieking at us to follow him. We refused, and, since he would not come with us, we went without him.

'Well, what a terrible time we had. Darkness was upon us long before we reached the foot of the peak. We arrived exhausted, injured and frostbitten. But at least we got home. Jack Laslett did not.

'Next day when the weather had lifted, they sent out a search party. They found him huddled beneath an overhang, frozen to death. But the worst of it, Doctor . . .' and here he hesitated, finding it difficult to make the admission, 'the worst of it was that Laslett's route down the mountain *had* been the correct one. Had we followed him, we might all have come home.

'Well, that is not quite the end of it. Laslett was married with one ten-year-old boy. When his wife heard the details of the tragedy she was sick with grief and fury. She wrote us the most venomous letters, accusing us of betrayal and cowardice and every other despicable crime imaginable. But she also promised to have her revenge upon us. "The worm of vengeance . . ." (these were her very words) "the worm of vengeance will find you wherever you go."

'Well, no man could but be shaken by such passion, especially when a shadow of guilt lies upon his soul. But, as the years passed, we came to forget Jack Laslett and his widow and never spoke about the business. Then, two years ago, a full twenty years after Laslett's death, McAndrew died in his library. He had apparently fallen against a bookshelf and split his skull. I was suspicious at the time, but my doubts turned to certainty when, six month's later, it was Thorne's turn. They found the poor fellow hanging from a tree in his garden. Nothing I could say would persuade anyone that these tragedies were incidents of murder, but I knew that Thorne would never take his own life. It became clear that Mrs Laslett would not stop until she had added me to her list of victims.'

'You never tried to meet her?' I asked.

'She had long moved away from her former home and no one could say where she had gone. I might have pursued her, but frankly I was afraid to get too close. I thought it more wise to shut myself away and barricade myself against her attacks. As you see, I have survived these two years, and I hope I shall go on a good deal longer.'

While Angel Holland told his story, daylight had given way to dusk. Through all the windows of the circular room the lights of Battersea and Clapham and all places around and beyond had begun to be lit. They sparkled now in the pool of darkness in which we seemed in our tower to hover, like travellers in a night balloon. 'It would, I imagine, be difficult to climb this tower from the outside,' I said.

'Impossible,' said he. 'It is quite proof against that, my boy, you can take my word. As long as nothing unauthorized comes up in that lift, I am safe enough. And if I am a prisoner in my own home, well, what of it? I'm fond of the place. Now you must let me retire. Come to talk to me in the morning.'

'I shall do that, Mr Holland.'

The old gentleman's story had effected me more than a little and, as I lay awake in the strange bed that night, it seemed to me that I had judged Angel Holland rather harshly. He was wholly convinced, however unlikely it might seem to others, that his colleagues were the victims of a remorseless vendetta, and I reflected that anyone might retreat from life who felt forced to live under such a sentence of death, against which there was no appeal, and for which there was not even a designated day of execution.

I spent the early part of next morning speaking to each of the servants, checking that they knew their routines for the day. Mrs Callendar the cook and Jethro the young coachman had adjusted quite happily to having a stranger act as their incumbent master. The housekeeper, Mrs Fowler, was, however, determined under no circumstances to make things easy for me. She expressed plainly her view that it would be a good thing when Thursday came around and young Mr Holland returned to restore the house to its proper order.

At about noon I took the lift up to the tower. Angel Holland and I smoked cigars while he entertained me with stories of his past exploits.

At about half-past twelve I whistled down the tube to Mrs Fowler to check that lunch would soon be ready. At precisely one o'clock I got into the lift, threw the switch and descended to the main hall. Mrs Fowler was there at the door of the lift. We exchanged a few cool pleasantries while we waited for the tray to come from the kitchen. This arrived a little late with Jethro, one hand under the tray and the other clamping down its rattling silver hood, arriving at a trot.

'Dressed crab, Doctor Watson,' said he chirpily, 'nice and hot. Some buttered toast, cold ham and pickle, fresh bread, soup. Decanter of wine in the basket. Watch the vibrations, sir.'

I took the tray into the lift, closed the door, started the lift and returned to the top of the tower.

At the summit, the lift door opened upon a small vestibule which gave directly onto the door of the round room. I knocked once and entered. The shock of what I found there caused me to throw up my arms. The tray flew from my hands and fell with a tremendous crash.

As I steadied myself and began to take stock of the situation, this is what I saw. One of the windows of the round room had been smashed utterly. Broken glass littered the room. Angel Holland lay on the floor, his eyes bulging from their sockets, his tongue protruding. His face was purple and he was dead.

As soon as I had come to my senses I had three things done. A wire was sent to Caspar Holland bidding him to return home immediately, and warning him that something serious had happened to his father. Another went to Sherlock Holmes, asking him to travel to Battersea immediately. And finally I had Jethro take a note to the police asking them to send a senior officer.

While waiting for the gentlemen in question to arrive, I

occupied myself with clearing up the mess made when I had dropped the tray, for it seemed to me that the shards of crab flesh and ham that littered the floor around the corpse served only as a macabre garnish to a scene already sickeningly grim.

The policeman arrived first, a tall, scrawny, sandy-haired young man by the name of Inspector String who had reached the rank of inspector somewhat early, and appeared to believe himself more than worthy of the honour bestowed upon him. He examined painstakingly the site of Angel Holland's death, studying in turn the floor, the broken window ('which,' he said, 'might be a deliberate artifice, of course'), the corpse and virtually the entire contents of the tower room. He made copious notes on a small pad which he carried in the pocket of his jacket, seeming to take no heed of any remarks I made to him regarding the circumstances of the tragedy. At last, after almost forty minutes in the tower, he asked me to convey him down into the house.

As we descended together in the lift, Inspector String studiously avoided my gaze, clearly determined to maintain me at a distance he considered appropriate to a murder suspect. I made a lame attempt to point him in the direction of the revenge plot which Angel Holland had sketched for me the night before his death.

'Twenty years ago, Doctor Watson? And the blood still hot?'

'It is not unheard of,' I replied, 'why, I have been involved with Sherlock Holmes in a number of cases in which the hunger for retribution . . .'

'All very dramatic, I dare say,' interrupted the policeman scathingly, 'but not commonplace. Did you know that an estimated ninety-three per cent of murders are committed by friends or families of the victims? Ah – I believe we have arrived.'

The lift stopped and I opened the door for him. There was some hustle and bustle in the hall. Mrs Fowler had just admitted a visitor whom she was escorting to the sittingroom, while Jethro ushered a second man into the hall and closed the door. Inspector String, jerking his head this way and that like some wading-bird whose territory is being usurped, called out to the housekeeper at once in a voice squawking with outraged authority, 'Mrs Fowler!'

'Yes, Inspector?' Her deference was absolute.

'I must be told who is entering and leaving this house. I insist upon being consulted before anyone comes or goes.'

'I'm sorry, sir. This is Mr Cuthbert, the lift engineer. The gentleman that just went through is, er . . .' she retrieved the card from her apron pocket and read it, 'is Mr Sherlock Holmes, sir.'

This news relieved me immensely.

'Ah, good!' I said.

String looked irritated. 'I will see everyone in the drawing room at once.'

Cuthbert, the engineer, appeared to be quite bewildered. 'What's going on, Doctor?'

'Mr Angel Holland,' I said, 'is dead. He was murdered this morning.' I described the details to him as we walked toward the drawingroom and he shook his head morosely, though whether from grief or merely at the threat to his means of livelihood, I could not tell. 'That's terrible,' he said, 'terrible.'

It was then that I spotted Holmes, and made my way over to him. 'Holmes, thank goodness you're here. It has been the worst afternoon of my life.'

'I came as soon as I got the wire.'

'I was supposed to protect him. I failed. What will I say to Caspar when he returns?'

'Is he on his way?'

'If he got the message. He may have been out on a climb, of course. Oh, it's a terrible business.'

'I dare say you did what you could, my dear fellow.'

When we were gathered together in compliance with the Inspector's dictat and stood awkwardly around the room – the servants, Cuthbert, Holmes and myself – String took up his position officiously before us. He leafed through the pages of his notebook for a few seconds then closed it ostentatiously and laid it with a small snap on the table in front of him, as if to demonstrate that he could summon us to attention with the minimum of effort.

'There has been a murder in this house,' he said, and then, somewhat tautologously, 'A man has died.'

Holmes, I noted was looking around the room, impatient to be out of the policeman's company and off on his own trail.

'I shall want to talk to each of you individually,' String went on, 'and then later on all together. So please do not leave the grounds. Doctor Watson, you and I will speak first. Perhaps you could remain behind?'

As the others began to clear the room, Cuthbert came across to me. 'Doctor, what do you think? While I'm waiting, should I go ahead and do the job on the governor-wheel I came to do? Or is it all pointless now?'

'Well, I dare say it will have to be done at some time,' said I, 'and if safety is involved, you had better go ahead. It will keep you occupied while you're waiting upon Inspector String's pleasure.'

Holmes had meanwhile been having a word with String, and now came to me. 'Our young inspector will not require to speak to me,' he said, 'so I shall take a look around the house. Meet me in the library when he has finished with you.'

My interview with String was a somewhat humiliating experience. The vehemence and rudeness of his questions allowed no precautions against the possibility of my being innocent. He belaboured me for an hour about my conversations with Angel Holland. Had the old man been rude to me? Had we argued? Had I invented the story of the worm of vengeance? On this last count, I assured him that Caspar Holland, on his return, would corroborate my statement, at which he asked whether Caspar and I had been friends for a long time, and what was the Holland estate worth, with the clear implication that he thought we might be conspirators in a murderous bid to annexe the Holland inheritance.

I made the library rendezvous with Holmes as soon as my ordeal with String was over. My friend, however, was more interested in assessing the man's capabilities than in commiserating with me over my bad treatment.

'He seems a thorough sort of fellow,' he said as we made our way to the lift, 'and sensible enough. He balked at first at my request to examine the scene of the murder, but as soon as I mentioned Kirby at Scotland Yard he became altogether more compliant. That shows a sort of pragmatic intelligence, I suppose, at least as regards his own career.'

Holmes was intrigued by the elevating machine. In his prolific reading he had already come across the name of Otis, and knew a little about the man's invention. As we rode up I explained to him about the arrangement that had prevailed while Angel Holland was alive – that no one should travel up and down except in the company of Angel's son, Caspar. He wanted to know every detail of all that had happened and, when I had given it to him, insisted upon going over everything again. The body, when we reached it, lay just as Inspector String and I had left it, gruesome in its death-mask of purple.

'So let us be clear,' said Holmes, 'you and Mr Angel Holland were together in this room until lunchtime, when you, Watson, went down in the lift leaving him here on his own. When you reached the hall below, you waited beside the lift with Mrs Fowler until the food tray was brought from the kitchen by Jethro, the coachman. You then came directly back up in the lift and opened the door of this room to find the window shattered and Angel Holland like this.'

'That is it exactly.'

'And there is no way into this tower except by the elevating machine?'

'None. Unless the assailant had wings. But you'll check for yourself, I'm sure.'

'I shall. You are fairly sure he died of asphyxia by strangulation?'

'Yes. It looks as though something were wrapped around his throat and tightened. This colouring of the face and lips and the protrusion of the eyeballs – well, you're familiar with the signs. He couldn't have done it himself unless by hanging. Yet no one else had the opportunity.'

'Except yourself, Watson.'

'That, I fear, is how String sees it.'

'Well,' said Holmes, 'let us go and look around the grounds

and inspect the exterior of the tower. Who knows – we may find something the fellow has overlooked.'

The air was clear outside. The sun was shining and the grass and trees were almost dried out after the constant drizzle of the last few days. We strolled around the three or four acres which Barrowfields commanded.

As I have said, from the rear of the house the full height of the tower was exposed. While the bottom third formed part of the fabric of the main building, the rest jutted above the roof spectacularly and somewhat grotesquely, with a silvery, shimmering effect.

'The walls are quite sheer,' said Holmes, 'What's more, the stonework is rounded and glazed.' He stopped. 'Watson, what is the matter?'

Something which had been in the back of my mind all day had shown itself in my expression. I did not want to declare it, but I knew that if I did not, Holmes, now that he was on the scent, would get it out of me by subterfuge.

'Caspar Holland,' I said, 'like his father, is a mountaineer.'

'I knew that you had come here because young Holland was off on a climbing holiday,' said Holmes, 'What of it?'

'He is a very good climber,' I said. 'Holmes – you don't think . . . ?'

'That he might have ascended the tower himself? Put your mind at rest, Watson. Even a first rate climber would be unable to ascend that face without driving holes into the surface, yet as you see it is perfectly unmarked. Even if he had ascended as far as that parapet, he would never have got beyond. It forms an impassable barrier to prevent anyone getting to the windows. No, that is not how it was done.'

'Then how?'

If Holmes was preparing a reply, I never got to hear it, for at that moment we spotted a plump figure beckoning to us from the door of the kitchens.

'I do believe it is Mrs Callendar, the cook,' I said.

'Then let us go and see what she wants.'

Mrs Callendar apologized for hailing us clandestinely from the garden. 'It's just,' she said, 'that, whatever that pompous young policeman might think, or our Mrs Fowler imply with her nods and winks, I know for sure it wasn't Doctor Watson that killed Mr Holland.'

Holmes had taken on that look of rapt interest that characterizes his most intense moments. 'What did you see, Mrs Callendar? Rest assured that we will make good use of any information you give us.'

Before she would say another word, the cook insisted on taking us down the stone stairs into the kitchen where we were seated at chairs around the large table. She checked both doors again before she spoke.

'It was this morning. I'd prepared luncheon for Mr Holland senior and the Doctor here. Jethro had helped me and Mrs Fowler was by the lift machine, waiting. Well, I know Doctor Watson must have already been in the lift at the time, because I heard Mrs Fowler shout to us, "He's on his way down, send it through," meaning the food tray. At that moment I remembered I'd not put a sprig of mint on the soup, a touch the professor likes, so I told Jethro to hold up while I popped out to the kitchen garden, just over there, sir, where you two gentlemen were standing just now when I hailed you. From there you can see right up the tower and, well, something caught my eye, there under the window, just a blur of something as it moved up onto that parapet and out of sight.'

'A man perhaps?' I asked.

'No, sir, nothing human. At first I thought it looked like the tail of a cat, but it was too thick for that. It wasn't until just an hour ago that it came to me. What I'd seen was some sort of serpent – a black serpent – or a gigantic worm. I don't understand it, gentlemen, but it must be connected. It was up there the moment he died.'

Holmes rubbed his chin thoughtfully. 'Thank you, Mrs Callendar. I'm sure it was connected. That is most helpful. Now, we had better let you get on.'

'Thank you, Mr Holmes. It's to be a large do tonight.'

'A large do?'

'Haven't you heard, sir? The Inspector wants us all to meet over dinner, servants included, and young Mr Holland if he's back, for he means to expose the murderer there and then.'

This provoked me uncontrollably. 'Melodrama!' I said. 'Cheap undergraduate theatricals!'

Holmes remained calm. 'Let us go along with the charade, Watson. It might serve our purpose. Besides, perhaps the Inspector will turn out to be right and there *will* be an arrest tonight.'

'I don't see how you can arrest a snake, Mr Holmes,' said the cook.

'It would not be the first time, Mrs Callendar,' Holmes replied, smiling.

As we walked through to the front of the house, I asked him what he thought of the serpent theory. 'Interesting in its way,' he said, 'what do *you* make of it, Watson?'

'Well, if we were looking for a worm of vengeance, we might have found one. And if the snake were of the sort which constricts, that could account for the manner of Angel Holland's death. But the problem is that one can't imagine how it could have been done, unless snakes can be trained to ascend sheer walls, break windows and pounce upon innocent victims. I think, all in all, we ought to abandon worms completely.'

'Not completely,' replied Holmes enigmatically. 'For the time being, Watson, let's not abandon the tail.'

At approximately seven o'clock Caspar Holland, who had received my wire on returning that afternoon to his holiday hotel at Elder's Edge, arrived at Barrowfields. It was left to me to break to him the terrible news of his father's death, a task which I fear I executed imperfectly, as is always the way of these things. He was, however, most gracious. He had guessed from the wording of my message that he might well find his father dead on his return, and appeared shocked, but not entirely surprised, to hear that the old man had been murdered. When he had been told all the circumstances, he absolved me at once from any blame. He was convinced that the curse under which his father had lived for so long had finally come to claim him.

The burden of grief, however, did not mitigate his fury at Inspector's String's presumptuous seizure of the kitchen for the purpose of the great banquet of revelations he was planning. Only my assurance that Holmes meant to make positive use of this bizarre last supper prevented Caspar from putting an immediate stop to the scheme, and when seven thirty came, he, Holmes, Cuthbert the engineer and myself, together with the three servants, joined Inspector String around the dining table as Mrs Callendar served the soup course.

'Will you be saying grace, Inspector?' asked Cuthbert provocatively.

'Are you aware, Mr Cuthbert,' replied String coolly, 'of the seriousness of this business?'

'Yes of course,' replied the other man, his dark moustaches barely concealing a smirk.

'Then please drink your soup while I proceed.'

It was a strange ritual, but we all obediently picked up our spoons and began, while String pontificated gloriously.

'In a case such as this,' he said, as though the unravelling of world-shattering ideas were a matter as simple to him as blowing smoke, 'the facts represent the mere surface appearance of the business.'

'And what of the rest?' Holmes enquired disingenuously.

'What distinguishes a professional from an amateur, Mr Holmes, is the degree to which the science of deduction is applied to the facts.'

How he had the effrontery to present Holmes with this bromide as though it were a revelation I will never know. My friend merely nodded, however, as if grateful for the lesson.

'Let us take ourselves back,' String continued, 'to this morning. It is fifty minutes after noon and there are two men in the tower – Mr Angel Holland and Doctor Watson. Doctor Watson goes down in the lift to collect the luncheon tray and on his return five minutes later he finds Mr Holland dead from strangulation. Well – what could be simpler? Doctor Watson must be the murderer.'

Soup spoons around the table were stilled and all eyes turned to me for a reaction.

'Didn't I say it was so?' Mrs Fowler whispered audibly to Jethro beside her.

'Ah. Well it was not so,' returned String jubilantly. 'That is what I mean about appearances.' He looked at me. 'Is it the case, Doctor Watson, that you dropped the tray of food on discovering the body of Mr Holland?'

'Why yes,' I replied, 'I did. The shock . . .'

'I was certain you had, for I found a fragment of crab against the skirting board, fairly fresh, not a day old. Yet, Doctor, had you dropped that tray *as a stratagem*, to convince us that the discovery of the body had surprised you, would you have cleaned up the mess? Of course not – you would have left it for all to see.'

'I say,' whispered Holmes into my ear with genuine surprise, 'this fellow is not bad.'

'But,' continued the Inspector, now wagging his soup spoon like a teacher's rule, 'if it was not Doctor Watson, who was it?' He looked from one to the other of the assembled suspects, causing eyes to drop downwards as he did so. 'Well, nobody could have entered that tower who was not a first-rate climber. Like Mr Holland's son Caspar, here.'

Caspar Holland started. Clearly he had not been expecting this.

'I dare say you thought you'd worked out the perfect plan, Mr Holland. Having arranged a fake holiday, you invite Doctor Watson to deputize as your father's bodyguard. But you arrange your holiday near enough to London for you to be able to disappear from your hotel in the morning, catch a train back to Clapham Junction to do your dirty work, and still return to Elder's Edge by late afternoon, in time to receive Doctor Watson's wire and establish an alibi.'

'This is an outrage,' Holland spluttered, white with anger.

'No one but a first rate climber could have ascended the outer wall of that tower, Mr Holland. And none but you stood to benefit from the death of your father, since everything was to come to you. Only you could not wait.'

At this point Caspar Holland jumped from his seat and would have attacked the policeman bodily, but that Holmes shot out a hand and locked the other man's wrist in his formidable grip.

'Mr Holland,' he said loudly, 'is not guilty of murder, Inspector String.'

'You are mistaken, Mr Holmes,' said the policeman, and beckoned to his constable. 'Pearce. Arrest the man.'

There was commotion as the constable took steps towards Caspar Holland. Everyone stood up. Soup plates tumbled. Mrs Fowler scuttled toward the door to retrieve one of them as it rolled.

'No!' It was Holmes' voice. 'Stop *that* man!' He was pointing toward the door of the diningroom at a figure with a bag sneaking towards the door of the room.

Mrs Callendar thrust out her foot and there was a crash as the man fell. She was on him in half a second, pinning him to the floor beneath her considerable weight. It was Cuthbert.

'This is your man, Inspector String,' said Holmes, 'and you nearly lost him.'

'Mr Holmes, I'd prefer you didn't interfere,' said String, but his confidence was shaken.

'Hear me out, please,' my friend continued. 'You began this exposition very well. The business about the dropped luncheon-tray was a fine piece of deduction. However, in your haste for a solution you became impatient with the details. It is true that Mr Caspar Holland could have hurried back to the house while appearing to be still on holiday, but an examination of the exterior of the tower would have told you that no one, no matter how gifted a climber, could have scaled that wall yesterday. Not, at any rate, without help. Whoever the killer was, he needed an accomplice. And indeed he had one. In Doctor Watson.'

'Holmes!' I said, scarcely believing what I heard.

'Of course,' Holmes went on, 'the good Doctor did not know he was an accomplice. Yesterday, when Cuthbert here went to do his repair work at the top of the elevator, he attached a rope to the lift cage, letting down the other end of the rope over the side of the tower. It was the one risk in his plan, that someone would see that rope before he had finished his

47

task. Unfortunately for Angel Holland, no one at that stage did.

'This morning, just before lunchtime, Cuthbert sneaked into the grounds and attached himself to the end of that dangling rope, having only to wait until it was time for Watson to come down in the lift to fetch the luncheon. As the lift descended, so, of course, the rope was pulled up, hauling Cuthbert up the side of the building. What you saw from the kitchen garden, Mrs Callendar, was no black serpent, but the end of that rope as it was whisked over the parapet. Having broken through the window and strangled Mr Holland, Cuthbert then went back through the same hole in the glass, took his grip on the rope and waited until the lift came up again with Dr Watson and the lunch inside. As it rose, it lowered Cuthbert to the ground. He then had but one task left – to unhitch the rope from the top of the lift-cage. Which is why he had arranged to be here today.'

'That's absurd,' Cuthbert objected. 'I came here today to fit a new governor-wheel. I told them.'

'And yet,' replied Holmes, 'when you arrived, that canvas bag of yours was all but empty, whereas now it is so bulky you can scarcely carry it. May we see the contents?'

Inside the bag was a huge coil of rope, strong and black. 'Ninety foot of rope,' said Holmes, 'makes a heavy bundle.'

'Well, then, Inspector,' said Caspar Holland, 'who is right? Mr Holmes or yourself?'

String knew when he was beaten. 'You are right, Mr Holmes. I jumped to conclusions. One should never do that. Constable, clap the bracelets on Mr Cuthbert, he is obviously as guilty as sin.'

'Oh,' said Holmes, 'and the man's name, I am sure you will find, is not Cuthbert, but Laslett. Do you remember, Watson that when Jack Laslett died on that mountain he had a ten-year-old son? Well, it may have been the mother who swore vengeance, but it was the son who executed it, even though it took him twenty years. When he found out, Mr Holland, that your father had installed a lift, he offered his services as an engineer, thereby assuring himself regular access to the

48

house and the tower until such time as an opportunity should present itself which, eventually and tragically, it did.'

After Cuthbert, or rather Laslett, had been taken away by String and his constable, the solemnity of the events of the last two days caught up with us. I helped Caspar Holland with the sad business of laying out his father's body, then Holmes and I took our leave, riding into the night with the great Barrowfields tower looming up behind us. I suspect that only the servants took any comfort that evening, finishing off the meal which Mrs Callendar had been inveigled to prepare, and the several bottles of vintage wine which Inspector String, in a moment of reckless confidence, had ordered up from the cellar.

3

THE PADDINGTON WITCH

One winter, there opened in Church Street, Paddington, a bread shop of legendary excellence, less than a mile from the lodgings I then shared with Sherlock Holmes in Baker Street, and it turned out that Mrs Hudson, the housekeeper who had served Holmes and myself so generously over the years, had a special connection with the shop's proprietors.

Kate and Bess Smullet were two sisters of roughly middle age, both unmarried, who had lived together all their lives. Within a week of their opening the shop in Church Street they were praised so assiduously in the neighbourhood that if you wanted bread from Smullet's before eight in the morning, you had better be there at sunrise. As a child, Mrs Hudson had attended the same school as the Smullet girls, becoming good friends with Kate Smullet, Bess being at that time somewhat sullen and self-contained, where Kate was outward-going and open-handed. So it was a great surprise to Mrs Hudson, twenty years on, to walk into the new shop in Paddington to find these two former acquaintances behind the counter.

From then on our bread and pastries were always purchased from Smullet's Bakery, and on the evening when this adventure properly began Holmes and I were at Baker Street, tucking into a pair of Smullet's Premium Quality Beef and Mushroom pies. The fire was lit, and we seemed to have successfully consigned the windy December night to the other side of our steaming windowpane. However, as I refilled his beer glass, I noticed Holmes picking somewhat peevishly at his food.

'My dear fellow,' I ventured, 'are you not enjoying your pie? Mine is excellent.'

'Oh, I have nothing to say against the pie, Watson,' he replied, 'it is a perfectly good specimen of its kind. I mean it has a substantial crust, a consistency which is fullsome without being turgid, and a generous proportion of meat. It is just that the combination of mushrooms with beef has never been greatly to my taste.'

Seeing my friend chipping rather boyishly at his pie-crust provoked a certain mischief in me. 'You will upset Mrs Hudson,' I said. 'She has to go all the way to Church Street to purchase these. They are considered a speciality.'

'Tell me then, Watson, what am I to do? Conceal it in the coal-scuttle?'

'No, no, my dear fellow.' I offered my now empty plate to him, 'I am quite sure I could finish it for you, if that would help.'

'Very kind, Watson.' Holmes tipped the steaming pie onto my plate. 'Of course, I am rather banking on the probability that after eating two of these you will have limited appetite for the cakes and pastries.'

At that moment we heard Mrs Hudson's short knock on the door and she came in to see whether we were ready for the next course. As she served us I noticed her looking at Holmes rather nervously, as if carefully choosing her moment to speak. The ludicrous thought occurred to me that she might have heard Holmes passing me his pie, and be about to remonstrate with him for it. Eventually she said, 'Mr Holmes, I'm not sure if this is the right moment, but I would dearly value your advice, sir.'

'About some domestic matter, Mrs Hudson?'

'No, sir. About another thing. If you wouldn't mind. A sort of a mystery, sir.'

'You do not mean you wish to *consult* me?'

'I suppose I do, sir. Though not in a fee-paying sort of way.'

'Oh, Mrs Hudson, please!' He laughed affectionately. 'You

surely know me better than that. Now please, sit yourself in the armchair and tell us what is the matter.'

And so she did. The first part you have heard, of her childhood friendship with the Smullet sisters, and their reunion in the Church Street bakery. But as she got to the next part of her tale she became quite agitated.

'I've mentioned to you that it was Kate who, at school, was properly my friend. Well, when they opened the bakery some six weeks ago they share the shopkeeping, and it would be sometimes Kate at the counter and other times Bess. I found Bess very different from the girl I remembered, for you'll recall that I said she could be almost sulky as a child. Here was a changed person, a merry, kindly soul, full of sympathy and glorious good humour. Hard to believe it was the same gloomy Bess I'd known from schooldays, except she looks much as she did then, plump as a new pumpkin.

'About three weeks ago when preparations for Christmas were everywhere underway and the Smullets were beginning to display Christmas puddings and mince pies in their window, Bess suddenly stopped serving at the shop counter. I missed her, for the truth was I'd grown to like her the better of the two. When I asked Kate about the whereabouts of her sister, I was told that she was unwell, and doing less work. Worse, that she sat in a chair in the parlour from getting-up to bedtime, would see no one, ate but little, and complained ceaselessly. I offered to visit her but Kate told me she would see no one. All this seemed very strange to me, as well as sad, but all I could do was to continue to visit the shop regularly in the hope of some better news, for which I pestered Kate on the occasion of my every visit.

'Well, good news there came none and, in the end, I lost my patience.

'"Kate Smullet," I said, "are we or are we not friends?"

'"Of course we're friends, Mrs Hudson," says she.

'"Then you must tell me the plain truth about what's going on here. I'm no fool, and I know when something is not right."

'Kate cast her eyes down, then said to me, "Very well, I'll tell you everything. But on one condition. You make no attempt to speak to Bess." I made her that promise, reluctantly, I must say, and here is what she went on to tell me, not a pleasant tale, sir, as you'll hear.

'When Kate and Bess opened their shop in Paddington, it was the fruit of twenty years of dreaming. They'd worked hard selling bread and pies out of trays and off barrows and, little by little, they'd saved enough to pay a deposit on the Church Street bakery. They could hardly believed their good fortune when it became an overnight success, but they'd barely had time to celebrate when events took a turn for the worse.

'At the opposite end of Church Street from the Smullet's shop is a tenement block. Locals call it the Smokey. You'll know it, sir, that old, black mausoleum of a place where kids fight with rats for crumbs of bread and there are more villains than privies. Pity the poor folk who have to call it home.

'Well, it seems that just after the Smullet sisters took their shop, two brothers moved into the Smokey, Garth and Saul Ransome by name. At about the same speed as the Smullet's had earned themselves a fine reputation in the neighbourhood, the Ransomes had acquired a wicked one. Their game was to go knocking upon the doors of honest tradesmen, demanding money, with a so-called accident promised to follow if it were not paid prompt. Well, most folk, out of fear, coughed up fast. Only Fairburn, the pawnbroker, refused to give them a penny, for which audacity his shop was burned to the ground and he was lucky to escape with his life.

'One day the Ransome brothers paid a visit to Kate and Bess Smullet. Kate wanted to pay up but Bess refused, said she would not be intimidated and sent the villains packing with some strong language and threats of the police. For a few days it seemed as if the brothers had backed off, but it turned out they were just biding their time.'

At this point in her story, Mrs Hudson stopped, apparently uncertain how much she ought to confide in us. 'Go on, Mrs Hudson,' said Holmes, encouraging her warmly. She took a breath and continued:

'Kate Smullet asked me to follow her to the kitchen next door where the baking ovens are sited. She guided me with a lamp, for it was already dark, and as we went she said, "I am going to show you something, Mrs Hudson. I want you to ready yourself for a shock."

'Set into the walls in the baking-room, were a number of small iron doors with big handles. These were the silos where they kept the various grains and flours they used for baking. From one of these, Kate slid back the lid. "There it is," she said.

'At first, in the half-light, it was hard for me to see inside. Then I could pick out the shape of something lying there in the dark, something black as the iron itself, but soft. When Kate moved the lamp closer, I saw it. It was a dog. I mean, it *had* been a dog, of medium size, but was now burned to a cinder.

'"Kate," I said, "what is this dreadful thing?"

'"Jacko was his name, poor mite" said she. "He was our Jack Russell. A good housedog, a strong barker, and to Bess almost like a child, I suppose. She doted on him. It was the Ransome brothers did this thing to the poor creature, Martha, because we wouldn't pay them, and may their black hearts rot for it, for I don't think Bess will ever quite recover."

'That's most of the story, Mr Holmes. There's a little more to tell. But I'm wondering if anything can be done before those brothers strike again. The Smullet women are in terrible danger, sir, and though I've informed the police, I fear they don't mean to act against the Ransomes.'

During the latter part of Mrs Hudson's tale, Holmes had lit a pipe and was now puffing at it.

'I will have a word with a senior policeman next time I am able, Mrs Hudson. You have my word. Now, you said there was more to tell?'

'Yes, Mr Holmes. I was back in the shop this morning, buying your supper and asking as usual after Bess, when Kate suddenly pointed through the shop window.

'"It's Garth Ransome," she says, "without his evil brother, for some reason. What does the villain want, I wonder?"

'The door opened and in Ransome walked, no taller than you, Doctor Watson, but very muscular and with a red-skinned, pugnacious look about him. His hands were fisted and he took a bully's delight in making the whole world quake in fear before him. There was no doubt he frightened Kate, though she did her best to stand up to him. She said, "We're open for normal business, Mr Ransome but, as you see, I've a guest here, and I can't discuss other matters." By which she meant, I suppose, the matter of paying him extortion money.

'But he didn't seem interested in that. "It's my brother," he said curtly, "he ain't too well."

'He put his bunched fists on the counter. "You told me your sister done a bit of doctoring on the side," he said, "Well you can tell her I want her to use a drop of her witchcraft on my brother."

'"Let's have no witch-talk here," Kate said, "it carries. As for Bess's gifts, it's true all right that, though she's no physician, she can soothe a cough and break the back of a fever."

'"And collywobbles," said Ransome, "you said she could put paid to that."

'Kate said that if he meant cholic, Bess could possibly help.

'"You tell her she's to come and take a look at our Saul," said Ransome, the danger in his eye daring her to refuse.

'"We've the shop to look after, Mr Ransome."

'"Later then. When it's shut. He's in pain and I want it stopped before his whining drives me to a violent remedy. Got it?"

'"Yes, Mr Ransome." says Kate, "she'll be there."

'"She better be" he said, and went out as fiery as he'd come in, banging the door behind him.

'I said to Kate, "But if you can't get Bess to leave her armchair, how will you get her to go and visit that pig of a man and his brother in the Smokey?" To which all she would say was, "I'll find a way."

'That talk of witchcraft has been playing on my mind, Mr Holmes. For I've been thinking, if she really *were* tied up with evil work, it might account for these sudden changes in her ways.' Mrs Hudson looked rather imploringly at Holmes. 'I'm confused, sir. What do you make of it?'

Holmes smiled. 'I shall make more of it, Mrs Hudson, when I know more facts. You provide insufficient data for any sure conclusion. But it is an interesting story and I shall give it some thought. I promise you.'

'Thank you, sir,' said Mrs Hudson. Then reverting at once to the role of housekeeper she began collecting the plates from our table.

'What do you think, Watson?' Holmes said, directly she had left us.

'Well, I can see why Mrs Hudson is puzzled. One minute Bess Smullet wants to shut herself away and see nobody, not even her friends, the next she is available to visit this Ransome fellow, of all people, with a cure. One might conclude she agreed to it out of fear except, of course, that she had already shown her defiance of these ruffians. One would expect her to wish him ill, not well. It does not strike one as natural behaviour.'

'And yet,' said Holmes, 'peculiar behaviour is no crime, and not often witchcraft. I fear we must leave Mrs Hudson to unravel her little mystery herself. Unless and until something else happens.'

With that, Holmes disappeared into his room and began to play his violin, a sign, I concluded, that he considered Mrs Hudson's story to be a trifle over which he would expend no more energy. However, before the sun was up next morning there were indeed new developments, and of a bizarre and distressing kind.

I had been lying awake from about four o'clock, unable to sleep. It had been a cold, damp sort of night and I recall reflecting what a terrible thing it would be to be out in that bitter, winter darkness. Suddenly I seemed to hear, very far off, a commotion of human voices, either laughing or screaming, so distant that I could not be quite sure whether they were real souls somewhere out there in that miserable night, or mere fantasms sobbing in the depths of my own dreams, as sometimes happens when one is half asleep, half awake. In fact, I did go to sleep soon afterwards, but not for long, because I was woken by an urgent knocking on the bedroom door. 'It's Mrs Hudson, sir,' a voice called. 'There's an emergency, Doctor.'

As a medical practitioner, of course, one becomes accustomed to being called out of bed at all hours. I always keep my medical bag near the bed, equipped with all the basic essentials, and am able to dress and be ready within ten minutes of being summoned. But when I left the bedroom I was surprised to encounter Holmes in the passageway, also dressed to go out.

'Holmes. You are up too.'

'Mrs Hudson seems to require us both,' he said. 'Apparently there is some odd business at the Smokey.'

There were no cabs in the street and the world seemed to have slammed its shutters fast against the bitter morning. Accompanied by Mrs Hudson, Holmes and I strode briskly in the direction of those grim tenements in Church Street. The nickname 'the Smokey', it was once explained to me, had arisen because of the tendency of its tenants to light fires at night in the central courtyard, a practice which caused smoke to billow in at the doors and windows of the apartments. The place was dreadfully run-down, and, as is so often the case, because its rents were cheap, it attracted mostly the poor and the desperate.

Moving at a brisk pace, it took us less than fifteen minutes to get to our destination, during which time Mrs Hudson explained what had alerted her to the emergency. Apparently, half an hour before, a boy of about ten had hammered on our back door asking for a doctor and saying that there had been 'witch-work' at the Smokey. This mention of a supernatural connection did nothing to cheer me on that appallingly grim morning for, as we approached the tenements, their dark, high walls did indeed seem to take on something of the appearance of a satanic fortress looming out of the morning mist. Indeed, what we were to find there was sinister enough.

The central courtyard around which the tenements are constructed provides for the tenants an area in which to hang out washing, as well as a forum for the trade of news and gossip. As we entered the yard, a large crowd had gathered at one end, while other tenants watched the proceedings from their apartment windows.

While Mrs Hudson loitered on the periphery of the throng, Holmes and I pushed our way to its centre, where a woman's voice was proclaiming loudly. 'He seen everything, that dog. Pity he can't talk.'

'He made enough racket last night, Doll Freeman' a man's voice replied, 'I thought someone was making sausages out of him.'

'You wouldn't be making small of it, Frank Bailey, if you'd seen what I saw. Besides, whatever sort of creature he might have been, a man met his end here last night. Show a bit of respect,' said the lady firmly.

By this time we could see her – a blonde-haired, fairly large woman of about forty, poor but bonny and neatly dressed. It was clear from the way she dominated proceedings that she was well thought of by her neighbours in the tenements. I wasted no time in addressing her.

'Someone called for a doctor,' I said. 'Can I be of assistance?'

'You're a bit late, sir,' the lady replied, 'Saul Ransome is well past doctoring, and besides, the coppers have just had his body taken off to the morgue, what's left of it.'

At this point, Holmes stepped forward. 'You say Saul Ransome is dead. May I ask you, Mrs Freeman, what you did see here last night?'

'And who are you, sir?' she asked boldly.

'My name is Sherlock Holmes.'

'Of Baker Street?'

'The same.'

'God bless us. My brother used to run messages for you, sir. Dick Archer, sir. One of your street lads.'

Holmes' face it up with sudden recollection, 'Young Dick! Ah yes, an excellent fellow.'

'Thinks the world of *you*, Mr Holmes,' she said, and then, with a hearty smile, 'Come into the room, sir, and meet my old man, and we'll tell you as much about this business as we know.'

Soon afterwards, Mrs Hudson, Holmes and myself, together with Mrs Freeman and her amiable husband Ben, were sitting in their cramped sittingroom while she made a pot of tea and described to us the events of the previous night.

'I take it you know this Saul Ransome, sir,' she began.

'Rumour has it,' replied Holmes, 'that he was in the extortion business.'

'And all manner of other nasty things. Well, anyway, him and his brother Garth live right above us here on the fifth floor, so we see the two of 'em coming and going on the stairs, all hours of the day and night.

'About three o'clock this morning, a banging door wakes me. Then there's a voice outside. It's Saul Ransome muttering to himself on his way down the staircase. A minute later I hear him in the yard below where he keeps that vicious dog of his chained to a kennel. Right, I think, he's feeding the little blighter, let's hope he don't make too much noise about it.

'Suddenly there's this great flash at the window, lighting the room up like a thunderstorm, and that dog begins yowling like a wolf at the moon. I wake Ben and we go dashing down into the yard thinking the poor creature is being tortured. But it's not the dog that's done for, it's Ransome himself, lying there in what's left of the kennel. Everything's burnt to a cinder, Mr Holmes. Everything – and him as well. His face is the only bit left that you could say was human – and the look on that ... I hardly like to think about it.'

We asked Mrs Freeman a number of questions but there was little she could add to her story and, having thanked her for her help, we returned to the courtyard where Holmes was keen to inspect the site of Ransome's death. Mrs Hudson left us to chat to some of the other folk in the courtyard, whom she seemed to know.

The corner of the yard where Ransome had died consisted of an almost bare plot of earth where one or two hardy weeds were struggling for existence. The first thing that came to my notice was a large, almost circular patch of burnt earth in the centre of the plot, around which were scattered blackened fragments of what had probably been a glass bottle and the charcoaled wooden remnants of the kennel. Holmes picked up one of these pieces, crumbled some of the timber in his fingers, sniffed it and sprinkled it to the ground like a pinch of black salt. Then he searched the area around his feet until he discovered what appeared to me at first to be a flat piece of fire-blackened card but which, as he inspected it and peeled away at it, I saw to consist of several packed layers.

'Paraffin oil,' he pronounced, 'was the agent of combustion. And there was a lot of it. And this,' he continued, waving the layered piece of burnt card, 'was the matchbox from which, more than likely, came the spark that sent the poor man to his death in a great fountain of flame. Mercifully, I doubt he felt very much.'

'Then he killed himself?'

'It is highly probable. It was a damp night. A trail of bootprints leads from the staircase over there to the place where Ransome died – but only one trail. How could a murderer have got near enough to pour paraffin over his victim without leaving footmarks? Also, someone employing such a volatile method of execution would need keep well back from his victim and to toss the match from as far as possible away from the impending conflagration. Yet the matchbox is here, where the man died. No, I am fairly certain Ransome died by his own hand. But as to why . . .'

'Perhaps,' I interjected, 'those stomach pains got to be too much for him, and he sought to escape his misery once and for all.'

'Well, Watson,' said Holmes doubtfully, 'it is a theory.'

Further speculation was put paid to by the sudden reappearance of Mrs Hudson, who seemed to be in something of a panic. She had with her a tall, gaunt woman dressed in a black dress with a white apron and bonnet, looking not unlike, I thought to myself momentarily, one of the early Quaker women.

'Mr Holmes, Doctor Watson,' said Mrs Hudson, 'I want you to meet Kate Smullet from the baker's shop. There's something she wishes to tell you. Something very troubling.'

'It's about my sister Bess, Mr Holmes,' said Kate Smullet, 'She was here last night, quite late.'

'How late, Miss Smullet?' Holmes asked.

'Well she left the shop at about ten, sir.'

'For what purpose?'

'To come and visit Saul Ransome. He was sick, sir, and he had requested her to come and deal with it. She knew something of herbal medicines and the like, you see, sir. But I'm frightened she might have done something terrible.'

'I see,' said Holmes, then, after a pause, 'What time did your sister Bess return home?'

'That's the point, sir,' said Kate Smullet, 'she didn't return. She's been gone ever since. You might say it's like she whirled away on a broomstick.'

That afternoon a most unusual tea party was convened at Wilson's Coffee House in Queen's Road. Its guests were Holmes, Mrs Hudson and myself, and it marked the first occasion of our taking refreshment together in a public place, Mrs Hudson being not entirely comfortable with the idea of a landlady eating out with her guests. But Holmes had wanted to go over the whole Smullet business in detail and felt that Wilson's genteel establishment would provide the ideal setting. A lot had happened since the death of Saul Ransome that morning.

We had not talked long to Kate Smullet about the disappearance of her sister Bess because she seemed too confused to answer Holmes' questions, and only wished to get back to open her shop. Despite Holmes' insistence that Ransome had died by his own hand, Kate was certain that suspicion would fall upon her sister, and indeed it did, for Garth Ransome let it be known that he was sure his brother's death had been the work of 'that witch Bess Smullet' who had visited him the night before. 'She blamed him for the burning of her dog,' said Ransome, admitting nothing, 'and she witched him to die of burning himself.' And then he'd added ominously, 'But she'll pay for it. She'll pay.'

The police did not know what to think but, keen to be seen taking an active part, promised to instigate a 'thorough and extensive search' for the missing Bess Smullet in order to question her in connection with Saul Ransome's death, a statement which led Holmes to comment wryly that whereas an ordinary police search would take a week to come up with nothing, a thorough and extensive one could take as much as a fortnight to reach the same conclusion, thus demonstrating its exhaustiveness.

Now, in the coffee-shop, Mrs Hudson was nibbling at a fresh scone and listening intently to Holmes.

'Mrs Hudson, it is my opinion that there are often two aspects of events. The surface can so easily seem to be the whole story, but only so long as one is not privy to the intimate, deeper view of the matter, an insight which often comes only with personal familiarity. Now, I wish to describe the events of these last few weeks according to the surface view and afterwards to ask you, Mrs Hudson, knowing the Smullets as you do, to make your own observations.'

'As you wish, Mr Holmes,' said Mrs Hudson, looking decidedly sceptical about the idea.

Holmes stirred some sugar into a cup of tea and continued. 'The Ransomes threaten the Smullet sisters but, because they get no money out of them, kill and burn Bess's pet dog. Soon after, Bess refuses to see anyone, leading to the speculation that she may be too busy dabbling in the black arts to have time to peddle scones and puddings. That she agrees to go and heal Saul Ransome of his stomach complaint adds to the suspicion of her occult powers. Soon afterwards, Saul himself dies in a fire and Bess disappears. Are not the implications obvious?

'Holmes,' I said, '*you* don't believe she is a witch, do you?'

'As I said, my intention is merely to present the surface picture – the one which the average observer, who did not know the Smullets, would immediately see. But you do know them, Mrs Hudson, so what say you?'

'I say,' said Mrs Hudson forcefully, 'that Bess Smullet is a good soul and a Godfearing woman, and ever was, even in her sullen childhood days. She is no witch.'

'That is your conviction?'

'Yes, Mr Holmes, it is.'

'Then we must look for another interpretation of these facts. Thank you, Mrs Hudson. And now I think we shall return to Baker Street.'

It had been late when we entered the coffee house and now, though only five o'clock, it was a dark December afternoon. As our cab trundled now along the eastern end of the Harrow Road towards Baker Street, the damp in the night air settled in droplets on the carriage window. We all three sat quietly for most of the ride, having just about talked ourselves out in the coffee house, until as we passed Paddington Green, I spotted a light among the trees, and a gathering of people.

'What is it Holmes, can you see?' I said.

'No, it is too dark.'

He called up to the cabby, 'Take us as near as possible to those trees,' and, within the minute, Holmes, Mrs Hudson and myself were running with the crowd toward the source of the excitement.

What we found there was utterly horrible. Although I have seen many corpses in my time as a medical practitioner, despatched in all sorts of unpleasant ways, I cannot recollect anything worse than this outside of battle. Stretched out stiff as a board was a human body, but one so blacked and charred with burning that the flesh had become papery on the outside and cooked beneath like well-done pork. Mrs Hudson, however, stared at it with awful recognition.

'It is Bess Smullet,' she said, and then quietly, 'Dear Lord.'

At that moment a man in flat cap, apparently recognizing Holmes, handed him a piece of paper which had been found attached to the burnt body. It was a note, and the pencilled wording on it proclaimed:

'THOU SHALT NOT SUFFER A WITCH TO LIVE'

'I think that is biblical,' Holmes said, 'though I could not give chapter and verse.'

'22 Exodus 18,' said Mrs Hudson confidently, 'and what's more I know who did this to poor Bess. It was Garth Ransome. In revenge for what happened this morning to his brother.'

Someone in the crowd shouted suddenly that the police were coming, and during that moment when the attention of the onlookers was taken away from the body, Holmes, who was kneeling over the remains, beckoned me.

'Watson, there is something here. Come closer.' We bent down next to the head of the corpse.

'Do you notice anything?' he whispered. I shook my head.

'Come along, Watson, you have seen bodies burnt on the battlefield.'

'Yes, of course.'

'And smelled them?'

'Ah! Yes, Holmes, I'm with you. That awful smell of burning hair and flesh. There is none of that here. An unnatural phenomenon!'

'Doctor, Doctor,' said my friend despairingly, 'why must you always jump to the remotest conclusion? If there is no smell, we must seek the reason why. But there's something else. Look. Inside the mouth. Something glinting. I want you to hold the teeth apart for me.'

'If I must.'

It was not a pleasant task. As I held open the blackened jaws, the flesh crumbled like burnt leather. Holmes inserted a finger into the shrivelled mouth, and found what he was looking for. Like a stage magician producing treasure out of thin air, he presented me triumphantly with two silver-bright threepenny pieces. 'There!'

'Good Lord!' I said, 'What on earth were they doing in the woman's mouth?'

'I believe the answer to that question,' said Holmes, 'would take us close to knowing everything, my dear fellow.'

Next moment running feet warned us that members of the local constabulary had come to claim the corpse as their own. Before we could be drawn into lengthy questionings, Holmes urged me to fetch Mrs Hudson from where she was exchanging theories in the crowd, and within minutes we were on our way back to Baker Street in the cab.

The following evening Holmes and I sat once again at the dining table in our Baker Street lodgings. I had been out buying Christmas gifts in Bond Street. Holmes, I guessed from the fog of tobacco smoke that issued from his room when he opened the door to join me for dinner, had been shut away all day, enjoying a long succession of pipes and ruminating on the matter of Bess Smullet's murder. A new cheerfulness in his manner suggested that he was pleased with his day's work.

'You are in fine spirits, Holmes,' I ventured.

'Yes, Watson. I am.'

'You've not heard the news?'

'What news is that?'

'Garth Ransome is arrested for Bess Smullet's murder.'

He smiled. 'Mrs Hudson informed me.'

'They dragged him away this morning,' I said, 'wildly protesting his innocence, of course.'

'Of course. But that's only to be expected, Watson. After all, he *is* innocent.'

'Ha! Well I believe, Holmes, you are the only one who thinks so.'

Yet although I scoffed, I had not, of course, forgotten that Holmes was seldom wrong in these matters. In fact, I was about to swallow my pride and ask him for his own views of the affair when Mrs Hudson came in with the food.

'Mushroom and beef pies!' she announced, as if introducing a celebrated music hall artiste. 'I told Kate Smullet how much you'd enjoyed the last ones, and she's just now brought these round, personal delivery, and won't take any payment.'

Holmes endeavoured to hide his lack of enthusiasm as Mrs Hudson put the plates in front of us.

'Mind you, Mr Holmes,' said Mrs Hudson, half-jestingly, 'Kate Smullet's a little cross with you at present.'

'Really? I have only met the lady once,' replied Holmes, 'I cannot imagine what I might possibly have done to offend her.'

'I was telling her you didn't think Garth Ransome had murdered her sister Bess. She says she's quite sure you are mistaken.'

'Well,' said Holmes, 'it is no doubt of some comfort to her to believe the matter is sewn up. Is she still with you?'

'She's staying here for the evening, sir. The poor woman's grieving terribly for her sister, you know. I'd better go down and join her, if you've everything you need.'

When Mrs Hudson had gone downstairs, Holmes reminded me that he had an evening appointment at the Old Bailey with a barrister friend. He offered me his pie and, when I declined it said, 'Well I cannot hide it, so I shall remove all traces,' then he wrapped it in a handkerchief and stuffed it into his coat pocket. 'Mrs Hudson,' he said, 'has quite enough on her plate at present without worrying about my appetite.' A few minutes later I heard his footsteps on the staircase and the slamming of the street door.

When I had finished my meal I went to sit in an armchair to read *Cranham's Magazine*. There was, I recollect, an article about skiing in the mountains of Austria. As I read I could occasionally hear the voices of Mrs Hudson and Kate Smullet in the room below, and it was at that point that the peculiar thing must have started to happen. I began to feel very cold and, dozing off, imagined myself to be upon a high and wintry mountain. I must have been only half asleep, for the voices of the women in the house persisted, but in my reverie they were on the mountain too, sitting on a distant peak, nattering happily, quite unaffected by the terrible cold. I wanted to shout to warn them of the danger of frostbite, but my voice was caught in my throat and I could not make a sound. A worsening pain in my stomach added to my miseries.

I managed at last to shake myself awake but the cold was still upon me and the pain in my stomach was fierce and real. Hauling myself out of the chair, I rang for Mrs Hudson. I told her that I was going straight to bed and asked her to bring me some morphine from my cabinet, to ease the pain.

A few minutes later she knocked on my bedroom door. I was, by this time, in my nightclothes and lying in bed, feeling appallingly cold.

'Did you bring the morphine, Mrs Hudson?'

'I didn't sir. I was talking to Kate. She says not to give morphine for stomach pain, sir.'

'Never mind what Kate Smullet says,' I replied tetchily, 'I am the doctor, Mrs Hudson.'

'Kate says there's a remedy her sister Bess used, sir, which will ease you in no time.'

And at that moment, to my surprise, Kate Smullet appeared behind Mrs Hudson in the doorway. 'Let me do what I can, sir. I promise we'll have you out of your discomfort in no time.'

I cannot remember exactly what made me agree to the woman's ministrations, but I think I was so beset with pain and cold that I would have agreed to anything to gain some relief and, certainly, there was something infinitely persuasive about Kate Smullet's voice. At any rate, before I knew it, she had sent Mrs Hudson downstairs and was sitting on a chair at my bedside. She put out the light and begun to talk to me soothingly in the darkness.

'You're cold, sir, I dare say.'

'Bitterly.'

'There's a frost upon your flesh. Deadly if it gets to the bone. We must prevent it.'

'How?'

'Why, with heat, sir. A heat strong enough to thaw the ice in the heart.'

It seems extraordinary to me, looking back, that I could have been beguiled by this mumbo jumbo, but although awake, I had, I am sure, only one foot in reality. Even as I listened to Kate Smullet's words, I seemed to be again on that mountain-top, only now in pitch darkness, and in that bitter cold and loneliness, this woman's sweet, sympathetic voice seemed my only companion. I remember her asking me if I had facilities for making a strong fire, and my replying that I had, if I could only leave the mountain and get to Holmes' laboratory. Taking my hand, she told me that she could lead me off the mountain and guide me there, a promise which filled me with overwhelming gratitude and happiness.

Then suddenly Kate Smullet was gone and I was alone among the retorts and burners and glass bottles of Holmes' room, feverishly, desperately trying to concoct something in a glass phial. The various fragments of knowledge I had accrued during my studies in chemistry and my time in the army seemed for the first time to cohere, and I found myself mixing chemicals of the most precipitous and volatile kind into a cocktail of devastating potential. Throughout this I continued to hear Kate Smullet's gentle voice in my head, instructing and encouraging me. 'Just put a flame to the fuse,' it whispered, 'and up it will go – and you'll have enough heat to heal everything' and I heard myself reply, 'Enough heat? Enough heat to blow the walls off the house.' Yet I continued until the thing was ready. The thing, I say. It was, I now know, nothing less than a bomb, a glass carboy packed with a cocktail of flammable materials with a short paraffin-wax fuse emerging from its neck. Yet though I held it in my hand and looked at it, I was only half aware of what it was I had made. To me it seemed to be simply the healing object that was needed.

I found myself putting a wax taper into the bench-side lamp and, with the burning end of it, touching the tip of the fuse on the carboy. The magnesium sizzled and I felt a surge of relief that my labours were done. I was sure that the heat in this con-traption would take away the cold and the dreadful pain in my stomach. In fact, I found myself taking hold of the round glass bottle as if it were a dear relation, embracing it, anticipating its healing warmth. The fuse hissed as the flame within it crept towards the explosive heart.

The flinging open of the door broke into my trance. A tall, dark figure was rushing at me. I knew immediately that his one desire was to steal from me the precious object to which I clung. He locked his arms around it to wrestle it from my grasp. I held tight and cried out. He shouted and pleaded with me but I was certain it was all a trick. I clung ever tighter. The sparks from the fuse had reached the bottom of the bottom of the bottleneck. At that moment the stranger swung out at me with his fist, dealing me a violent blow to the jaw and, snatch-ing the carboy out of my arms, hurled it through the glass of the window. There was a huge explosion outside. Then darkness came down upon me like a black canopy.

Early the next morning Holmes, Mrs Hudson and myself found ourselves once again together in a cab. I had passed a strange night, with repeated nightmares about windy mountain-tops giving way at last to a deep and peaceful sleep. Holmes, for, of course, it was he who had wrestled the incendiary device from my grasp and hurled it through the window, had remained at my bedside until he was certain the fever had passed.

He insisted, however, that we rise very early. Mrs Hudson, in low spirits herself, was prevailed upon to make us tea, which Holmes insisted I drink in large quantities.

'It will flush the poison out of the system, Watson.'

'Poison?'

'You'll recollect that I took away in my pocket last night one of Kate Smullet's beef and mushroom pies. Well, it was a fortuitous act, and fortuitous too that I was at the Old Bailey when the thought occurred to me that those pies might be the key to this whole business. I abruptly terminated my appointment and dashed around the corner to Bart's, where I was to find my old colleague Ashleigh Harcourt still at work in his laboratory. You remember him, Watson, a brilliant chemist. My haste turned out to be a wise one. The mushrooms in that pie you ate last night were in fact a lethal mixture. Apart from normal, edible mushrooms there were two sinister varieties included in the recipe. *Russala emetica*, "the sickener", to provoke the nausea and stomach pain and, more deadly yet, the fungus *panaeolina foenisecii*, which induces, among other things, hallucinations, feelings of being persecuted, and extremes of physical sensation such as heat, cold, pain, ecstasy.'

'Kate Smullet did that to me?'

'It was nothing personal, Watson. She feared we knew too much and were in her way. She meant it for both of us. The plan was, as you know to your cost, to persuade us to destroy ourselves with fire.'

'Just as Bess Smullet did to Saul Ransome. So both the sisters are in on these black deeds.'

'Bess Smullet could not have done anything to Saul

Ransome, my friend. She was already dead. She had been murdered. In fact, one might say she had the rare distinction of being murdered twice.'

'Holmes, what can you mean?'

'When you have finished your tea, Watson,' Holmes said with huge satisfaction, 'we shall visit Kate Smullet at her baker's shop, and then you will know everything.'

It was still early when our cab drew up outside the little bread shop. The street was dark and empty, but a heavy frost gave to the road and pavements a snow-strewn aspect, and with that and the spectacle of holly and mistletoe in the neighbouring shop windows, there was the feel of Christmas in the air. My nightmares of the previous evening seemed far away, and although my head was still fuzzy from the experience, I felt a twinge of excitement as Holmes, Mrs Hudson and I approached the shop. I was intrigued to meet Kate Smullet again and to see whether Holmes really would be able to resolve the whole business.

It being only four thirty the shop was yet locked, but a light within indicated that Kate Smullet was up and about already, as bakers must be, preparing dough for the ovens.

Holmes knocked several times on the door until eventually Kate Smullet opened up for us. I thought I noticed a flicker of fear pale her face when she first saw me, but she did not permit it to linger. Holmes explained that it was important that we spoke to her immediately to clear up certain matters and, although she complained that she had her work to do and had little time to spare for chit-chat, she agreed to let us in. Mrs Hudson and I sat on chairs in the small sittingroom at the back of the shop, while Holmes paced about.

'Doctor Watson is alive, Miss Smullet, as you see,' said Holmes, stridently laying his opening card.

'So he is, sir,' replied Kate Smullet cannily, 'despite his being so poorly last night, but then it isn't often a man dies of a bellyache.'

'On the other hand,' said Holmes, 'it is rare for a man – or woman – to survive a fireball.'

At this point, Kate Smullet tried a different tack. I'll have you remember, Mr Holmes, that I am still grieving for my poor sister Bess, freshly murdered.'

'And I'll have you remember,' Holmes riposted, 'that her murder is not as fresh as all that.'

'Two days, sir.'

'More like a month, madam.'

'Are you implying something, sir?'

'That you have not been as solicitous of the truth as you might have been, Miss Smullet.'

At this, Kate Smullet seemed to spit fire. 'Mr Sherlock Holmes,' she said, her eyes black with anger, 'I warn you, sir, not to press me on this. Out of this shop, sir, and off with you. And you too, Mrs Hudson, and the doctor here. The consequences won't be good if you rouse a demon in me.'

Mrs Hudson backed towards the door, chilled by this outburst, and I confess that I too was taken aback at the sight of this small woman transformed into a raging fury. Holmes, however, stood his ground.

'If you are threatening us with magic, Miss Smullett, I had better warn you that you will need a lot of it to deflect me from my determination to see this matter out. Sit down. And you too, please, Mrs Hudson. Then you shall hear the entire story.'

The authority in Holmes' manner cowed Kate Smullet. We all seated ourselves in silence and waited for Holmes to continue.

'I do not know,' he said, 'whether Kate Smullet had been planning the murder of her sister for years, or whether it happened spontaneously. At any rate, about four weeks ago, while the Smullets were preparing the mixture for their Christmas puddings, Bess was murdered.'

At this, Kate Smullet started with surprise, as if Holmes had been able to read the deepest recesses of her memory.

'She was killed by suffocation, her head pushed into a bowl of Christmas pudding mixture and held there until she stopped breathing. Which, of course, is why her body was found with two threepenny pieces in the mouth. She had sucked them in while fighting for breath.

'As for Jacko, the dog, well, he had to be disposed of too, for a dog will sniff out its mistress, dead or alive, and that might ruin the entire game.

'Miss Smullet attempted to dispose of these two corpses in the bread oven. There, although they singed and charred badly, they would not incinerate. Such an oven is not hot enough to destroy such a density of tissue. She was left, therefore, the proprietor of the charred remains of one dog and one human being, a grisly merchandise indeed, and one whose disappearance had to be expedited as quickly as possible.

'In the meantime, Mrs Hudson, she strove to persuade you and other regular customers that Bess was still alive, inventing that nonsense about her being unwilling to see visitors.'

'But then, if Bess was already dead, who killed Saul Ransome?' I asked.

'Why, Kate Smullet here, of course,' said Holmes. 'It was an essential part of the plan. The Ransome brothers bought, or were given, one of Miss Smullet's poisoned pies. It did not matter which Ransome ate the poison, the other was fairly certain to come to Bess for help, since Kate had let it be known her sister could cure stomach pains. Then, masquerading as her sister Bess, Kate visited Saul Ransome and, in the same way she hypnotized you last night, Watson, she sweet-talked him into setting himself alight in the courtyard at the Smokey.

'Of course, the brother played into Kate Smullet's hands by swearing revenge, and when Kate Smullet deposited her own sister's charred body on Paddington Green, she made sure there was a note attached pointing to Garth as the obvious suspect. But Garth could not have set the body alight. You'll recollect, Watson, that it gave off no odours of singed flesh or hair, which it certainly would have done had not the burning been done many days before.'

'But Kate,' said Mrs Hudson softly, 'why did you want to kill her?'

'I admit nothing,' the other woman replied, 'but I tell you this, Mrs Hudson, I'd had my fill of the woman. When we were girls, it was *I* was the favourite. Then as we got older she wanted more and more of the limelight, playing up to every-one with her nice-as-pie ways until they all adored her. What a lovely woman is Bess, they'd say. What a kind soul. What an angel. Anyone'd get tired of that in the end.'

'And yet to kill – twice – for jealousy . . .' said Holmes, gently shaking his head.

'I admit to no murder,' said Kate Smullet.

'Nevertheless,' said Holmes, 'I must warn you that before we set out, I sent a note to the police asking them to be here at five, so you had better be ready for them.'

Kate Smullet suddenly looked infinitely weary, perhaps with the terrible realization that events had hemmed her in.

'Well then, sir, I had better go and turn down the ovens,' she said, 'if you will give me a few moments. Don't be alarmed. There's no back way out, as Mrs Hudson here will confirm.'

Kate Smullet never returned to her sittingroom. A few moments later we heard a roar from the baking-room which we took to be the sound of the ovens being vented. But when the woman did not reappear we investigated, only to find that she had thrown herself head-first into the furnace. It was a most distressing end to a terrible business.

And so it was that Paddington lost a good bread shop and Mrs Hudson a good friend, and I joined Sherlock Holmes among the ranks of those foresworn never, under any circum-stances, to eat another beef and mushroom pie, no matter how fresh.

4

THE PHANTOM ORGAN

Buried among the notebooks whose contents have, over the years, been distilled into those few handfuls of adventures which detail the methods and triumphs of my friend Sherlock Holmes, there exist some pages which it has always caused me a degree of pain to recollect. The tale I am about to recount is drawn from such troublesome archives, yet it is because I now see that it exhibits many details of singular fascination that I have decided at last to try and set it down.

There is, at one end of the Devon village of Windwhistle, a pretty little church called St Simeon's, large enough to seat only thirty worshippers, but charming in its way. It has a tower, but this feature is without internal walls, serving as it does to accommodate the staircase of the small organ gallery. Above the gallery is the short projection of the tower proper, with a window at each compass point. I provide these details because, as will become clear, St Simeon's, Windwhistle, is very much the centrepiece of the exceptional events I am about to describe.

I had become familiar with the village, however, and with its quaint church, long before those events began, for my first wife, Mary Morstan, had a cousin, Cordelia, who had married a clergyman, James Partridge. After a period of working as missionaries in South America, the Reverend Partridge and his young wife had settled down as incumbents of St Simeon's in the little cottage that stood opposite the church across the lane. In the years following our marriage, during which Mary and I spent several brief but pleasant holidays in that house, I came to be fairly well acquainted with James and Cordelia Partridge, but following my wife's untimely death, I gradually lost contact with them. Some places resonate so poignantly with tender memories that they become virtual furnaces of grief for the bereaved. So it was with Windwhistle and me. Had not circumstances drawn me back against my will, I should never have returned to the village at all.

However, one evening a letter arrived for Holmes by messenger. It had come that day via Exeter from one Lord Alistair Hembury, a high court judge who knew of Holmes' work through previous investigations. On this occasion the gentleman's request was of a personal nature. He required my friend to travel with all haste to Windwhistle, where the Hemburys had their family seat and where a dreadful incident had befallen them.

As Holmes and I drove next day to catch the Exeter train, I explained to my companion what I knew of Windwhistle and that this visit would be my first since Mary's death. He urged me to remain in London if the prospect of a return to the village was too painful for me, but I knew that he particularly required my medical opinion in this case and I decided that the moment had come to break the taboo. It was a fine, spring morning. As the train raced through the sunlit Wiltshire countryside I began to feel confident that I had made the right decision.

From Exeter we took a four-wheeler out along the winding lanes to Windwhistle. Just before we reached the village, the driver drew the vehicle off into a side road and, a little way down, through the iron gates of a long driveway. We continued for another quarter of a mile before Hembury Hall, an imposing, grey manor house, emerged from a cluster of trees.

Lord Alistair Hembury met us in the driveway, a large, solemn man in his fifties, with thick, grey hair, a military bearing somewhat compromised by good living, and a rather overweening manner. He did not bother to thank us for troubling to answer his call so promptly, seeming to presume upon our compliance as merely the degree of deference required for a man of his rank and importance.

'I dare say you'd like some tea,' he said, 'but that must wait. I wish you to see the phenomenon right away.'

With this cryptic remark, he led us into the basement of the house and along a passage to a heavy, oak door, unlocking which, he ushered us in. The familiar, sickly-sweet smell of embalming fluid told me that this was the family morgue and, sure enough, lying in a corner of the room upon a bed of black silk sheets was 'the phenomenon' – the horribly mutilated body of a man.

'My brother,' said Alistair Hembury, 'what's left of him. Bit of a mess. Found in the stables. Horses seem to have stampeded while he was feeding oatmeal biscuits to 'em. Couldn't get out, I suppose, once they started to rampage. Beeston, our local quack, reckons a snapped rib pierced his heart. Maybe. But that's not the whole story. If it was, I wouldn't have sent for you.'

I saw Holmes wince slightly at the notion he could be 'sent for' like some private in Lord Alistair's personal army.

'What's the rest of the story, then?' he asked.

'Mr Holmes, there has been a smouldering resentment against the Hemburys in this village for decades. It is, I suppose, the underdog's envy of the pack-leader. We run things tightly here. There are those who despise us for it.'

'You *run* the village?' said Holmes.

'We ensure that the rule of law and standards of decency are upheld here. It doesn't always make us popular. Mr Holmes, my brother was quite certainly murdered in a naked act of spite. Here's your evidence.'

He produced from his pocket a sheet of paper upon which was scrawled, in large charcoaled letters, a brief text.

'Some villain,' said Hembury, 'nailed it to the noticeboard of the church three days ago.'

The words on the crumpled sheet said:

'NOW IS THE HUNTER HUNTED H.H. SHALL BE FIRST'

Alistair Hembury waited until Holmes and I had looked over the document before he continued. 'But the night my brother died something even more astonishing happened in Wind-whistle. The church was quite empty, yet local folk swear they distinctly heard the organ being played. It was a thing called "The Post-horn Gallop" – some popular hunting song.'

'I believe I know the piece,' said Holmes.

'My own mother, Lady Hembury, who lives in this house, heard it herself. What's more, there was definitely a light in the church tower. Yet Partridge, the vicar, insists the place was locked. I suppose it is some abominable prank.'

'A wicked prank indeed,' said Holmes grimly, 'that ends in murder.'

Lord Alistair stared at the piece of paper again, seeming for a moment less sure of himself. 'Now is the hunter hunted.' He read the words in a mournful voice. 'That means us, you see. The Hemburys. We've been hunters for generations. Then "H.H. shall be first." That was Hugh.'

For an instant he looked quite pale and vulnerable, but the moment passed swiftly and he became business-like again.

'I expect you'd like to take a closer look at it.' He gestured to the body on the black bed. He did not appear to bear it much affection. 'Take your time. When you've finished, you'll find me in the parlour where you can give me your conclusions. Here's the key. I'd be grateful if you'd lock up behind you.'

'Conclusions,' said Holmes after the judge had gone, 'It's a little early for those. But one thing is clear – the Hemburys are a dying breed. Now that this one is dead,' he nodded toward the corpse, 'Lord Alistair and his venerable mother are the last two left.'

He stopped short. He was leaning close to the man's chest. At least a couple of ribs had been broken. White bone-ends were jutting through the breast and the local physician's diagnosis of death from a punctured heart certainly looked most probable.

'There is nothing here which your medical knowledge would tell you to be out of the ordinary?' asked my friend.

'Frankly, Holmes, no. There is a terrible look upon the fellow's face – but being trapped in a stable with rampaging horses would account for that. Were it not for Lord Alistair's suspicions, I'd hazard this to be a genuine accident.'

'Well, perhaps it is. But when you have finished your examination and we have "reported" to Lord Alistair, we had better investigate this business of the phantom organ, prank or not. And who better to talk to about it than your cousin-in-law and her vicar-husband? I wonder would they welcome a visit?'

In fact, to my surprise, Cordelia Partridge was initially more put out by our arrival upon her doorstep than her husband, who was thoroughly welcoming, inviting us immediately to dine with them. It was the sort of generous enthusiasm (I reflected later, when I realized there were no servants in the house) which comes more easily to one who is not going to be responsible for the cooking. When Cordelia heard, however, that we were considering putting up at the village inn, she immediately insisted upon our staying in their spare room, an offer which, after a little gracious resistance, we gratefully accepted.

Thankfully, the house had been rearranged since the days of my holidays there with Mary. What had then been the guest room was now occupied by the Partridges, reprieving me from at least some of the turmoil of memories with which the place threatened to besiege me.

Having deposited our overnight bags, Holmes and I descended to the large downstairs room where the Partridges and a hearty meal awaited us, as well as a good supply of the local cider. Holmes carefully avoided any direct reference to the recent incident at Hembury Hall, confining himself to questions about South America and listening to a number of the Partridges' favourite anecdotes. We were well into the meal when James Partridge himself introduced the topic which Holmes had been tactfully skirting around all evening.

'Frankly, we shall be glad of your company, gentlemen,' he said, 'I suppose you know about the strange business of the organ?'

'Indeed,' replied Holmes, 'Lord Alistair mentioned it.'

'It disturbed us both terribly,' Partridge said.

'James is being kind,' said his wife, 'It was I who was disturbed. Terrified might be a more accurate word.'

'Take a look out of the window,' said Partridge.

Across the lane we could clearly see the door in the side wall of the church. Its small tower, seen from our perspective, projected from the right-hand end of the building.

'As you see,' Partridge continued, 'the door is in full view. It is the only way in, and I am quite certain the building was empty, but a light shone in that tower as bright as a new moon, and we heard the organ play for a good half-minute, some profane, infernal tune.'

'How very intriguing,' said Holmes quietly.

It was twilight. Despite the beauty of the evening sky beyond the church, a tremor of fear moved me as I contemplated the scene of these singular events.

'But it's not just the organ,' said Cordelia. 'There was that awful warning nailed to our noticeboard and Hugh Hembury's subsequent death at the stables. The Hembury family has trodden upon people for too long. Now the evil they have done is coming back to them.'

'You make it sound as if you believe it to be some supernatural phenomenon, Mrs Partridge,' said Holmes.

'I don't know what I believe, Mr Holmes. But there is little love in this village for the Hemburys. They have their way in all things. During the last two years it has become quite intolerable. Even a vicar's wife is not exempt. Each evening, Mr Holmes, I am "summoned" to Hembury Hall where I am expected to listen patiently to her ladyship's complaints and tribulations and to attend to her every whim.'

'You are compelled to do this?' I asked.

'If I do not,' replied Cordelia, 'I cannot be sure that some poor soul in the village will not be evicted from a cottage, or some struggling farmer deprived of his living. The death of Hugh Hembury will not be widely mourned. It may even bring some good.'

'Cordelia!' said her husband.

'Forgive me, James. It was a tragic business. I should not have said that.'

The Reverend Partridge, apparently embarrassed by what might be perceived as a degree of impiety in his wife's views, endeavoured to hide his blushes, and was at that precise moment saved by a knock upon the door.

'That will be old Jennifer,' said Cordelia, leaving her chair, 'Excuse me, gentlemen.'

The front door of the cottage opened directly from the sitting-room onto the lane, enabling us to see the new arrival. She was an old woman in rather poor-looking black clothes, augmented here with a purple scarf, there with a sprig of broom, to give her, overall, a cosy and somewhat Bohemian aspect. Her face, rotund and rosy-cheeked with the vitality of the outdoor life, nevertheless told in the pattern inscribed in its wrinkles a story of considerable hardship and sorrow. There was about her an air of kindliness tinged with melancholy.

At first, seeing that the Partridges had guests, she offered to return on another occasion. Cordelia, however, would not hear of it, and persuaded the old woman to come in and meet us.

Her name was Jennifer Farway, a local whose family had lived in Windwhistle since time out of mind. 'Much longer,' as she put it, 'than they Hemburys.'

Cordelia explained that Jennifer had lost both her husband and a son in the last few years, and now made a small living baking sweetbreads. It was these she had come to deliver in a large basket covered with an immaculate white napkin.

'Jennifer's husband Joshua was a fine craftsman,' said the Reverend Partridge, 'It was he who built our organ here.'

The old woman turned down her eyes. 'Aye. Pity he were never paid for it.' Then she looked plaintively up at Holmes and myself. 'But I doubt you gentlemen have time to waste listening to an old woman's lament.' She began to unpack some of the goods from her basket onto the dinner table.

'On the contrary, Mrs Farway,' said Holmes, 'I should very much like to hear your story.'

The woman stopped and turned to Holmes with a grateful smile. 'Would you, sir?'

'I would. Really.'

'Sit down, Jennifer,' said Cordelia kindly, 'and tell Mr Holmes and Doctor Watson all about it.'

So the old woman took a seat at the table and, placing her hands in her lap, recounted the following tale.

'It were her up at the house – Lady Hembury – that asked Joshua to build the organ. "It'll be my gift to Windwhistle parish," she told him in her haughty way. Well, as you may imagine, gentlemen, we were never wealthy, yet not a ha' penny did she put up in advance. Joshua and I borrowed and scrimped and starved ourselves to pay for the materials to build that organ. And when it were finished, and everyone had admired it, and Mr Cassidy the organist had declared it played like celestial pipes, Lady Hembury laid down just half what monies she'd promised.

' "But, your ladyship," says Joshua, "that's barely enough to pay what I owe."

' "Times are hard, Joshua," she says, "Be thankful for what you get."

'Well that were that. What can poor folk do against the likes of them? But I tell you this, if it was only the money they owed me, I could let it go. It's the rest I cannot forget. And that's a fact.'

At that, Jennifer Farway stood and picked up her basket from the table. 'Have you a few pots for me today, my dear?' she asked Cordelia, who then opened the cupboard and began to fill the old woman's basket with jars of honey.

'We keep bees here now, John,' Cordelia explained, with much innocent delight. 'In fact – we make a little of our living from selling the honey. Windwhistle honey is praised throughout the county, you know. Jennifer here makes honey cakes with it. We trade with one another.'

When the transaction was completed, Cordelia and Jennifer Farway kissed fondly and the old woman went on her way.

'She is a sad character,' remarked Partridge as Cordelia closed the door behind the visitor.

'An honest, woman, though, I think,' said Holmes.

'Oh, completely so,' Partridge replied.

'I wonder what she meant,' continued my friend, 'when she said "if it were only the money, I could let it go."'

Cordelia and her husband exchanged glances, then Cordelia said, 'Well, you ought to know it all, Mr Holmes, I suppose. After that business with the payment for the organ, Jennifer's husband Joshua began to slander the Hemburys in public, spreading the word that for all their high blood they were dishonourable, mean folk who reneged on their debts and could not be trusted. People knew this already, of course, but it alarmed the Hemburys to hear it openly declaimed. They told Joshua to hold his tongue, and when he would not, they threatened everybody else in the village. No one was to employ him – though he was easily the best carpenter in this part of the county – on pain of reprisals. And I'm afraid their tactics paid off. It was a terrible thing to see. When Joshua could find no work, he took to drink. He declined faster than any man I've ever seen. He began to look more and more wretched and in the end, one night, he was found in a ditch, dead from exposure. That is what the Hemburys owe Jennifer Farway – the life of her husband.'

'Good Lord,' I said, 'Poor soul.'

'Yes,' said Cordelia, with tears in her eyes, 'poor Jennifer. And now, gentleman, you must forgive me if I leave you together. My evening appointment with the irascible Lady Hembury will not wait.'

'The truth is,' said Partridge, when his wife had gone, 'that we are all slaves to Lady Hembury's whims.'

Although Holmes' gaze was directed towards the vicar, his eyes seemed to be staring inward in a fever of concentration. 'No one has yet explained,' he said, 'what happened to Mrs Farway's son – except to say that he, too, died.'

'You are a very persistent interrogator, Mr Holmes,' said Partridge. 'Yes, there was something. You know by now that the Hemburys are great ones for hunting. Well, Jordan, the Farways' boy, rode once or twice with the hunt.'

'A carpenter's son?' I asked, surprised.

'It was a privilege the Hemburys liked to extend to certain of us "commoners" from time to time, all part of their feudal manipulation of our village life. Unfortunately, Jordan Farway fell from his horse at Itley Brook and was killed. It's understandable that Jennifer blamed the Hemburys, especially after what had happened to her husband, but I'm sure this was nothing other than a straightforward riding accident.'

Holmes, having considered this answer, appeared to be about to launch a supplementary question when, quite suddenly, we all froze, as a chilling sound shattered the quiet of the evening.

Organ music was playing in the church and, when we turned to look, we saw that there was a light in the tower which certainly had not been there seconds before. In the failing twilight it made an awesome sight, and the effect of that normally jolly melody, 'The Post-horn Gallop' emanating from a church organ in the middle of the evening, was so singular that our voices dropped to whispers.

'But we've been sitting at this window all evening,' I said, 'No one could possibly have entered the church.'

'No,' said Holmes, 'they could not. Mr Partridge, the keys of the church, please, quickly. And wait here, if you will, while Watson and I investigate.'

Armed with the keys, we rushed out of the cottage and across to the church. As Holmes turned the key in the lock, the music ceased abruptly in mid-phrase and as he opened the door the building was in darkness. There was certainly no light in the loft. In fact, the depths of the gloom compelled us to ascend the stairs of the tower with a certain amount of caution, and when we reached the organ-gallery, we found nothing.

'The organ is locked,' said Holmes. 'What is more, it has been locked for days. See? There's a layer of dust upon it, quite undisturbed. Have you the key on that bunch Partridge gave you?'

'Yes, I think this is it.'

'Open it please.'

Holmes played a few notes.

'What do you think, Watson? Does it sound the same as before?'

'I think not,' I replied, 'less – well, less haunting, perhaps.'

'Yes. Supernatural fingers clearly play a different kind of music.'

'It is odd,' I said, 'that there's not so much as the smell of a snuffed candle. No smoke. Nothing.'

'It's an extraordinary business, all right,' said Holmes, 'and so far, I confess, it has me baffled.'

Suddenly there was a noise below, a shadow moving in the depths. The door of the church opened slowly. Then a voice whispered 'Watson – Mr Holmes. . . .' It was Partridge. 'You'd better come down. I've found something.'

When we had all three returned to the house, Partridge put before us on the table a crumpled piece of paper similar to the one which Lord Alistair had shown us earlier that day.

'I found it just now, on the noticeboard, just like before,' said Partridge. Holmes read it aloud.

'*A.H. SHALL BE NEXT*'

'A.H.,' said Partridge, 'must mean Lord Alistair. He is in danger, then.'

'He might be,' said Holmes.

'Then I suppose we had better warn the man,' I said.

'I shall do it myself immediately,' said Partridge, 'and I shall bring Cordelia back from Hembury Hall at the same time. I'll not have her there with such things going on.'

I cannot say he sounded too confident that he would be able to persuade Lady Hembury to part readily with her companion but, as it happened, within the hour both he and Cordelia had returned to the cottage, and in a state of some excitement.

'There is pandemonium at the hall,' said Partridge, almost as he came through the door. 'They are in terror for their lives. Lord Alistair is talking about going away entirely. His mother, her ladyship, is begging and pleading and threatening him not to leave her under any circumstances. They are pacing this way and that like beasts in a cage, pulling their hair and rubbing their hands. An epidemic of fear has descended upon that house, gentlemen. In the end it was decided that Lord Alistair would depart for his rooms at Bristol Assize court first thing tomorrow and remain there at least until the end of the month.'

'Well,' said Holmes 'it is too dark to make any more investigations tonight. Perhaps tomorrow, Reverend Partridge, we could look around the churchyard and gardens?'

'By all means, Mr Holmes. And I hope you will stay here at the cottage for as long as you need.'

When we had retired to our room, Holmes sat on the bed with his chin in his hand. 'It is all very elusive,' he said. 'Not least the business of Hugh Hembury's death. You will not be shaken from the conviction that he died from crushing?'

I reiterated that I was certain this was how he had met his end.

'Yet,' he said, 'it presents us with this problem: how could a murderer plan a death by stampede? Too much is left to chance in such an escapade. A horse may or may not stampede, even when provoked, and even a stampeding horse may do no damage. Moreover, the risk to the murderer might be as great as that to the victim. As for this business of the phantom organ, it has quite got me beaten. No more than five seconds elapsed between the time that music ceased and the moment we entered the church, yet there was nothing at all there, indeed I am certain no one had been there for some time.'

'We have two mysteries, then,' I said, 'the mystery of how Hugh Hembury was murdered, and the mystery of the phantom organ.'

'Well, yes,' replied my friend, 'if Hugh Hembury was indeed murdered. And if his death was an accident, we have the mystery of how the phantom organist could have predicted it. On the other hand, of course, if the organist really is a phantom,' and here, Holmes gave a chuckle, 'then there is no mystery at all about how he got into the church, for phantoms, I believe, are credited with the facility of passing through walls.'

'You don't believe that to be the case, of course.'

'It would be a rare phantom that composed items for the church noticeboard,' said he, 'But I must confess, Watson, that at this moment, I do not have a better theory.'

The following morning we woke late, for the excitement of the previous evening had kept all four of us talking until well after midnight. The cottage being so small, Holmes and I set out for a long walk to allow the Partridges a little time together, returning just before noon to find them both busy in the church garden. It was a fine morning and Cordelia seemed in good spirits, despite the unexplained events of the night before.

St Simeon's stood in three acres, two of which were given over to the graveyard. A path separated this burial ground from the third acre, the Partridges' garden, which backed onto the church itself, their cottage across the way having no land of its own. The beehives of which Cordelia was so proud stood in a row along the path, protected from the wind by a line of yews, but the strangest object in the entire garden, not visible from the cottage, was an old, Romany caravan tucked in against the side of the church building, its paint faded and its woodwork showing signs of rot. Holmes remarked upon it immediately, and the Reverend Partridge beamed with delight at the opportunity to rehearse again the story of its origins.

'It's been there for years, Mr Holmes, ever since my predecessor played host one summer to a family of travelling people. There had been a series of unfortunate incidents in the lives of these wanderers. First, they had fallen out with their community, who were fairground folk, and had struck out on their own. Then the father of the family had become sick and unable to work. The old reverend put them up for six months, during which time he was able to make contact with some distant relatives of the family on the Isle of Man. These people had accommodation and were willing to provide their cousins with a permanent home, and the family decided to accept the offer and settle down. They left the caravan where you see it now, with vague ideas that at some time they might retrieve it, but they never did. It has stood there against the church wall ever since, and fearing to move it, in case one day they come back for what is theirs, I suggested we should put it to good use. Cordelia now uses it as an apiary, for the husbandry of a certain delicate variety of bee. I fear, though, that the weather will claim it before very much longer, and I don't like to paint it, for, as you see, it is decorated in a traditional manner and would be a shame to spoil, even to save the woodwork.'

The caravan did, indeed, appear to be in a very delapidated state, yet it must have been delightful in its day, the shuttered windows painted gaily with elaborate, floral designs. Much care had once been lavished upon it.

'Holmes,' I said, as we wandered the garden together, 'do you think it possible that someone might be using that caravan as a shake-down, and somehow sneaking into the church to play the organ?'

'Even if he were, Watson,' said he, 'I don't see that it would answer our problem. The church windows do not open. A glance will tell you that they are impenetrable. There are no holes in the walls, and no ways of getting under them. In short, there is one way and one way only into the building, and that is through the door which faces the Partridges' cottage. Whether our phantom resides in the caravan, travels regularly down from London by train or returns nightly to one of the graves in the churchyard, we still have not explained how he could get into that church and out again, leaving no trace whatsoever of his having been there. But,' continued my friend, in a more positive tone, '*this* is interesting.'

From his pocket he drew what I took at first to be a shred of burnt paper but which, on closer inspection, proved to be a charred fragment of very fine linen. 'It was here next to the church wall.'

'It might have been there for years.'

'I think not. There are no signs of weathering.'

'You have a theory, then?'

'No, Doctor, not anything so concrete. But I am forming one by degrees.'

At that moment, Cordelia called to us to look towards the lane. As we turned our eyes upwards, a smart, black landau was speeding by, out of the village and toward the Exeter road.

'It's Lord Alistair,' said Cordelia, 'off to hide himself away in his court chambers.'

Despite the bright weather, the hood of the carriage was up and the window curtained, with the driver, a ruddy-faced man in a red-spotted neckerchief, driving the horses at a good pace, as if the occupant could not wait a moment longer to get away from Windwhistle and its lurking dangers.

'We'll have luncheon,' said Cordelia, her eyes sparkling with something like relief at the departure of the gentleman from the big house. 'Windwhistle will be a nicer place this next month without that man.' But we were to hear of Lord Alistair Hembury again much sooner than that.

Twenty minutes later, when we had just sat down at the table to take our soup, there was an urgent hammering at the door of the cottage. The Reverend Partridge opened it to find himself confronted by the driver of the landau, his red-spotted neckerchief now gripped in his hand, mopping his brow in a state of distress.

'Reverend Partridge – for mercy's sake – something terrible's come about. It were nothing to do with me, Reverend, I swear in God's name.'

'Where, Giles?' asked Partridge.

'Just half a mile along the lane. It's Lord Alistair, Reverend. I think he's dead.'

Partridge insisted that Cordelia should remain at the cottage, but he, Holmes and myself, together with Giles Derriman the driver, made our way along the lane to where the vehicle had stopped, slewed off to one side as though it had been brought to a sudden halt. Derriman, who opened the carriage door for us, turned out to have made an accurate diagnosis, for his former master was certainly deceased.

'We were going along apace when I just heard him shout, Reverend. Like in pain. Or surprise, maybe. I called back but he never replied, so I stopped. And this is how I found him.'

Lord Alistair Hembury lay slumped in the narrow space between the facing seats of the carriage, his head thrown back and his features fixed the most ghastly expression of terror. Without touching anything, Holmes took a careful look about, then sniffed the air twice.

'Cigar smoke. Yes. See? He had just lit one.'

He leaned inside and retrieved a cigar from the floor. It was no longer smoking, having apparently burnt itself out when it fell upon the man's cloak, where there was a deep scorch-mark. The cigar-box was upside down on the seat, with the remainder of its expensive contents scattered about the interior.

'Have a look, Doctor. See if you can ascertain the reason for this man's sudden demise.'

Examining the body as thoroughly as I could within the awkward confines of the landau, I found no obvious cause of death. We knew the end must have come quickly if Giles Derriman's story were accurate, for only seconds had elapsed between Lord Alistair's cry and the discovery of his corpse upon the carriage floor. This pointed most obviously, in my view, to a heart attack or a stroke.

'Do you think it was fear that did for him?' Partridge asked me.

'It is certainly true that fear can, in extreme cases, cause the heart to fail,' I replied, 'yet, according to Mr Derriman here, Lord Alistair seems to have been in no immediate danger, nothing that would set the heart palpitating excessively.'

'Then it is odd,' said Partridge, 'that he should have died so soon after that threat.'

'You think,' said Holmes, 'that he was still in the grip of our phantom?'

'It is that or a most sinister coincidence,' said Partridge. 'But how can a man be killed remotely?'

It was a long day. After the Reverend Partridge had gone off to summon the authorities prior to making his way back to his wife, Holmes and I waited for the message to reach the police in Weighcastle some sixteen miles away, for their representa-tive, an Inspector Wolfe, to arrive, for the local physician to confirm my diagnosis of heart failure, and for the only undertaker in that part of the county to muster his transport, a hay-wagon roofed and painted black into a make-shift hearse. We also spent a good hour searching the lanes and hedgerows for a hundred yards behind the spot where the landau had finally stopped, to see whether any clues had fallen out of the carriage in the time that had elapsed between Lord Alistair's sudden cry of alarm and the subsequent discovery of his corpse. However, as it turned out, all this waiting proved worthwhile, and on several counts.

When Addiscombe, the undertaker, needed help to move the body of Lord Alistair Hembury into his hearse, the task of assistant bearer fell to me. It was as we laid the corpse on its back to slide it headlong into the black wagon that I noticed the dead man's ankle, which had upon it a small swelling in the shape of a whitened circle, slightly cratered in the middle. At the centre of that crater was a tiny perforation.

'Look Holmes,' I said, 'this is interesting.'

'Is it a needle-mark?' asked my friend.

'Possibly,' I replied, 'Do you think he might have injected himself with an overdose of some narcotic?'

'I would think it possible if there were any way for him to have disposed of a syringe. But we have searched the area quite thoroughly. No, it is not that.'

At this point Wolfe, the policeman, asked to talk to Holmes, so I took a turn up the lane, sat for ten minutes upon a pretty bridge watching the water, then made my way back. This was when the second piece of fortuitous information came my way. Holmes being still engaged with the police inspector, I asked Giles Derriman, who had also resigned himself to an irksome and mostly wasted day, what stretch of water I had just visited. In fact, had he not been in so restless a humour, I doubt whether he would have disclosed to me all that he did.

'They call it Jameswater now, Doctor, but its ancient name is Itley Brook.'

The name rang a bell. 'Isn't that where Jennifer Farway's son Jordan fell and was killed in the hunting accident?' I asked.

Derriman scoffed. 'Who told you that yarn? Jordan Farway never died in no fall, Doctor. He were hunted down and killed. Everyone in Windwhistle knows that, even if nobody dares speak it out.'

'Did you say hunted?' Holmes, who had now finished dealing with Wolfe and had come across to join us, had caught Derriman's last few words.

'Yes, sir. After old Joshua Farway were found dead of drink in a ditch, his boy Jordan vowed he'd recover every last penny Lady Hembury had kept back from his father for the organ. One night he went down to Hembury Hall to take what was owed, and what happened next is so wicked it blackens a man's heart to speak it. The Hemburys caught him breaking in. They kept him locked in a cellar till they'd massed a hunting party. Then, Lord help us, they set the lad loose in Harpford Wood, like some animal, and chased him with hound and horse till fatigue drove the poor soul to ground. He were found at Itley Brook as you say, Doctor, but not from no fall. There were an arrow through his heart.'

'An arrow!' said Holmes.

'Oh they like their ancient weapons. All part of their airs and graces. Word is, it was Lady Hembury herself as led that pack, but no one who rode out that day admits to seeing no arrow fired, nor to pulling no bowstring.'

As Giles Derriman spoke, I had begun to be haunted by intimations of similar events from the past, but at the mention of the word 'arrow' such a strong sense of recollection overwhelmed me that I could no longer concentrate on what he was saying.

'Excuse me, Mr Derriman,' I said, interrupting him somewhat rudely, 'Holmes, a word with you.'

We stepped aside, close against the hedgerow. The sun was low in the sky and as we stood together in the lengthening shadows, I said, 'Holmes, you remember that business of the sign of four.' The reference was to one of the earliest adventures we had shared together, during which, in fact, I had become engaged to be married to Mary Mortsan, Cordelia Partridge's cousin.

'Every detail,' said Holmes.

'I was thinking of the blow-pipe and the poisoned dart,' I continued, 'Could not such a weapon be the very thing that killed Lord Alistair? The murderer would merely have had to lie in wait somewhere along this lane until Lord Alistair passed through on his way to Exeter. It was common knowledge he planned to go. A dart through the window of the landau might have done for him in seconds.'

'I confess,' said Holmes, 'that a dart, in poetic terms at any rate, is the perfect weapon of vengeance for Jordan Farway's murder. But when one considers the circumstances, one sees that it could not possibly be so. First, no dart was found, either upon Lord Alistair's body or in the carriage. Secondly, the curtains of the landau were drawn, and it is unlikely a dart could have penetrated them. Third, even assuming it could, it would certainly not have struck Lord Alistair *in the ankle*. Not, at any rate, unless he had been travelling with his foot dangling from the window.'

I had no choice but to accept this total immolation of my theory. 'You are quite right, Holmes, the idea is ridiculous.'

'Not ridiculous, Watson, merely incomplete.'

I got no more out of him, however, because Inspector Wolfe, who had now completed his investigations, decided at that moment to take his leave of us. As he rode away I noticed, to my surprise, that it was almost nine. We had been in that lane for almost eight hours and hunger, thirst and fatigue were taking their toll. I said as much to Holmes, who agreed that we should make our way back to the cottage. We stepped along the darkening lane that led back to St Simeon's, whose tower we could already see over the tops of the trees.

As we strolled together, Holmes spoke.

'Whoever is behind these extraordinary killings, Watson, appears to be having a good deal of wicked fun. Each time a threat, a haunting, and a murder, all painstakingly and elegantly executed, leaving no trace – not, at any rate, until today, when you found that mark upon Lord Hembury's ankle. This business is so audacious that clues should be falling into our laps like plums in autumn. Yet the whole thing remains so shrouded in mystery that one could almost believe. . . .'

'That there really is some supernatural force at work?' I suggested, tentatively completing his ellipsis. But he was not listening to me. His attention had been captured by the awesome sound now borne to us on the evening breeze. There was music from Windwhistle church, the same galloping music as before. Holmes pointed upward. 'Look, Watson. That light's in the tower again. Come along, quickly.'

But, as we hurried around the bend in the lane which led back to the vicarage, strange things seemed to be happening to that ghostly light.

'Holmes,' I said, breathless as we hurried along, 'it is floating out of the tower, floating to the ground!'

'Indeed it is. But how utterly stupid of me not to realize before – it was never in the tower, Watson. Look at the shape of it. Do you not see what it is?'

'How could I? I have never met the like.'

'Nonsense. It is a balloon. A toy hot-air balloon. Did you never make them as a boy? A sheet of light fabric stretched over a framework of sticks – set a candle on the cross-piece and light it – and the hot air takes it up and up, bright as a little moon. No, there never was a light in the church on those nights of the so-called phantom. The light was *outside* the church. We did not realize it because the tower always stood between the light and the vicarage. Sitting in the cottage, we looked into the tower window that faced us and out through one on the other side that faced away. The light, floating there, created perfectly the illusion of being inside the church.'

'It must have been anchored to the ground, then.'

'Yes. By a string, I suppose. Easy then to pull down, dismantle, extinguish, while the tower was being searched.'

'So that piece of burnt fabric you found. . . .'

'A perennial problem with candle-driven balloons. A tendency to catch fire.'

By this time the light had descended out of view and, as we came around the corner to the church, there was no sign of it at all. The music, however, continued a little longer, almost, in fact, until we reached the church building, when it suddenly stopped.

'It's almost as if he'd seen us coming,' I said.

'The organist? I think not, Watson. His tune always ends at the same place. Would you like to meet him?'

He led me to the door of the old Romany caravan. We were both panting after our run, but he signalled me to be calm.

'There may be danger in here. Remember, it is a beehouse. Gently now.'

He opened the door with as little noise as possible, though its rusty hinges squeaked. As we stepped over the threshold, a low humming greeted us, coming from somewhere inside the pitch-dark grotto that was the caravan interior.

Holmes struck a match. 'Look!' He pointed to a large, mechanical contraption which occupied most of the floor. It was some sort of fairground hurdy-gurdy, operated, it seemed, by clockwork. From its mouth, like a long tongue, a reel of perforated paper, similar to those used on domestic piano–organs, snaked outward.

'Of course,' I said, 'how obvious! A mechanical organ.'

'Yes, Watson, obvious now that we see it. On the nights of those hauntings our phantom had much to do. First to attach the doom threat to the notice-board of the church, then to scuttle behind the church here, light the balloon and float it up to the window, then to set in motion the music. As soon as the organ was started, he would have pulled down the balloon and been on his way.'

'Ah – you forgot to say – having first stopped the organ.'

'No. He had no need to do that. Watch.'

He passed me the match-box and asked me to keep a light going, then, lifting a red lever, pulled the paper reel a little way out of the jaws of the machine. Printed across the width of the reel was a line of large holes.

'These allow the brake to engage,' he said. He proceeded to demonstrate. As he depressed the red lever again, the clockwork jumped back into action, sucking the paper reel into the maw of the organ so that the familiar tune, deafeningly loud in that little caravan, assailed us for a couple of seconds until the large braking-holes had engaged again, when the noise immediately ceased.

'Ingenious,' I said, 'and so simple.'

'Yes. We assumed we heard the organ from inside the church, because that was where we thought we saw the light. We were doubly deceived.'

'That is the haunting explained, then,' I said, 'But why would anyone go to the bother of creating such an illusion?'

'That is indeed the key remaining question. But we'd better not stay here. We must check the church noticeboard.'

Thankfully shutting the door on that dark little bee-hole, we made our way to the front of the church. The Reverend Partridge, who was standing there beside the noticeboard, seemed relieved to see us.

'Watson – Mr Holmes – you heard the organ?'

'Yes,' I said.

'You had better look at this, then.'

These were the words to which he drew our attention.

'M.H. SHALL BE LAST'

'That' said Partridge, 'is Lady Hembury herself. Maude is her first name. It seems it is her turn now. She is in a terrible way, for she knows now that her son is dead. My wife was with her all afternoon, but could not comfort her – and now this. She will have heard the organ. She will know it is for her.'

'Your wife is up at Hembury Hall now?' asked Holmes.

'Not now. Lady Hembury sent her away. She is here in the cottage. Her ladyship has apparently locked herself in the armoury and forbidden anyone, even a servant, to enter. You had better come and join us in the cottage. You must be starved.'

'No,' said Holmes, 'thank you, Reverend, but there's something we must see to immediately.'

As Holmes and I walked briskly along the lane towards Hembury Hall, I was determined to get as much from him as possible.

'Do you think the killer is at the hall now?' I asked.

'Well, Watson, that is a question which requires a delicately honed answer. I am almost sure the killer is there, but I think the murderer is probably not.'

'What? How can that be?' He smiled and did not answer. 'Holmes,' I pressed, 'am I right in thinking that our culprit might be Jennifer Farway.'

'She is the obvious *prima facie* suspect, indeed, for not only had she lost both her husband and her son to the whims of the Hemburys, she also had an attachment to the church organ that might have made all this phantom business an appropriate sort of retaliation. But, unless she is more lettered than she pretends, I cannot see her as the author of those deadly epigrams pinned to the church noticeboard.

'Now, Watson, we are approaching the house. There might be some danger, so we shall stay together. Be on your guard, and be ready for a fight.'

The unequivocal desire of the servant who answered the door was to shut it firmly in our faces. Holmes, however, having foreclosed this option by inserting a foot between the door and the jam, proceeded to demand to see Fenton, the butler, who took it upon himself to admit us, though not before he had been chastened by Holmes' insistence that Lady Hembury's very life depended upon immediate action.

Once inside, however, we were at something of a loss as to how to proceed. The Butler told us that her ladyship had fallen into a state of abject terror. 'She's shut herself away in that room with all the old weapons. There's even a musket loaded and primed. Personally, I'd leave her until the danger has passed. At least no killer can get to her there. There are no windows and only the one door.'

'I'd be grateful,' said Holmes, 'if you'd show us to this room at once.'

The panelled door of the room proved to be of stout timber. When the butler knocked upon it, the noise resounded colossally around the hallway and up the broad staircase. 'Lady Hembury,' he called, 'Mr Holmes – the detective from London – wishes to speak to you.'

The voice that came back was menacing. 'Away with you, man. You have interrupted my supper.'

'But, Ma'am, we must think of your safety.'

'Away with you, I said!'

Fenton gave a petulant shrug as if to say he had done all he could. Holmes, however, wanted to know how her ladyship could be eating supper when no one had been able to take food into the room.

'Oh, she took something in with her, sir,' the man replied, 'Some fruit, a box of sweetmeats, a bottle of tea.'

'Then,' said Holmes immediately, 'we must get this door open. Can it be unlocked from without?'

'Are you thinking something in that picnic might be poisoned, Holmes?' I asked.

'You are nearer the mark than you know,' he replied.

The butler was fumbling through a bunch of keys uneasily. 'This could cost me my job, Mr Holmes.'

'And if Lady Hembury dies,' said Holmes, 'who will pay your wages then?'

Holmes grabbed the key that was handed to him, inserted it in the lock and opened the door, revealing Lady Hembury sitting in a large, ornate armed chair facing us, the musket in her lap. She looked up in fury as we entered, a wild, figure, grey hair in tangled disarray about her head, eyes staring, mouth open. We had caught her in the act of opening a neatly wrapped package, such as those in which good sweetshops sell their wares. A blue ribbon lay discarded at her feet.

'Lady Hembury,' said Holmes firmly, 'please put that box down.'

'Get out of here,' she spat, 'at once.'

'I must insist,' said Holmes, moving closer, 'that you give me the box.'

She swung the barrel of the gun towards us and I thought for a moment that she would fire outright. Holmes and I shrank backwards, covering our faces, but at that moment Lady Hembury gave a frightful shriek as something black and uncannily fast shot out of the package she was holding and swooped about her head with a huge, terrible droning. At first I thought it was some exotic breed of bird, but then I saw it clearly. It was a bee-like insect of immense size, a good four inches from head to tail, and its only purpose in the world at that moment seemed to be to attack the unfortunate woman who had released it.

As soon as she recognized what awesome thing was circling her she began to cry out. The box fell from her lap, cascading coloured sweetmeats this way and that across the floor. She swung the musket around in a futile attempt to target her tormentor. It dived at her, circled her head, dived again. The musket went off. Plaster hailed from the ceiling.

'The wall!' Holmes yelled to me. Crossed swords, shields and pikes hung around the walls in pompous ceremonial pastiche. We each grabbed a weapon, I a pike and Holmes a sword, and we set about attacking the huge creature as it dived and droned about her ladyship's head. For a while it would not be distracted from its chosen victim, but eventually began to recognize all of us as its enemies, swooping from one to the other in menacing skirmishes. Our weapons were useless. Yelling to me to keep the creature busy, Holmes rushed back to the wall, this time bringing with him a shield.

'Are you all right, Watson?'

'So far!'

'Capital!'

From the corner of my eye I watched him wedge the end of his sword through the handle on the back of the shield and begin to swing the thing like a great round-headed bat. It must have been extremely heavy, but Holmes's phenomenal strength made it seem designed for the job.

The first few swings failed to make contact, merely provoking that great humming creature to bolder and bolder forays, attacking me directly in the face, causing me to swing my own weapon wildly. Then, purely by chance, the very end of my pike nudged it. It swooped away toward Holmes as though I had bowled in his direction a fast-moving cricket ball. He was ready for it. Swinging his arms around his head he brought the shield-end of his weapon with a huge smack against the insect's body, sending it hurtling across the room. It collided with the farther wall and dropped to the floor.

Holmes quickly grabbed the sweetbox and rushed to where the creature lay. It was badly broken, either dying or already dead. Using the end of the sword to transfer it back into the box, Holmes replaced the lid firmly. 'In case it is needed for evidence,' he said.

We were all three exhausted after the ordeal. Lady Hembury, the worst affected, collapsed into her chair, white as a ghost and while Holmes returned the weapons to their wall brackets, I, reclining upon a lounge, tried to recover my breath. It was in this tableau that we were discovered by the Reverend and Cordelia Partridge who now came rushing into the room.

'John,' said Cordelia, in a high state of agitation, 'Mr Holmes. You are all right?'

'Yes,' said I, 'but it was a close thing. Cordelia, there was a giant insect, and had it not been for. . . .'

'Mrs Partridge knows all about the insect,' said Holmes, interrupting me, 'it was she who put it in the sweetbox earlier today.'

At the moment Holmes said these words my eyes met those of the Reverend James Partridge. I might have been looking into a mirror, for he and I reacted identically and simultaneously, our jaws dropping in utter disbelief.

'Mr Holmes,' began the cleric, preparing to mount a spirited defence against this slander of his good wife, but Cordelia stopped him calmly. 'It's all right, James. Mr Holmes is right. I did put the creature in the box. But I should like to know how he guessed.' Her husband collapsed completely dazed, into a tall chair and, like a man subjected to an unpleasant dream, attended helplessly as Holmes spoke.

'Well,' said my friend, looking at me, 'in a way it was your speculation about blowpipes and poisoned darts Watson, which first put the idea into my head. The little mark on Sir Alistair's ankle was indeed like a dart wound, but only a dart which knew its way could have found its target in that moving carriage. Now what is a bee, seen from a certain perspective, if not an intelligent dart?

'So, can a bee sting kill? Well, the answer is that there is no common species of bee which carries a fatal sting, except to those with a marked sensitivity to its venom, a very rare condition. But in our room at your cottage, Mrs Partridge, you had left a certain number of books about bees. Browsing through these the other night I learned of experiments conducted by South American natives in culturing hymenoptera from disparate species in an attempt to increase honey-yield, a process rumoured to have produced a giant species with a venom so deadly and so swift as to be almost instantly fatal to human beings. The name given to this creature was *vespa venatica* – the hunting wasp. I should have realized immediately what was going on, but I did not. It was not until this afternoon in the lane that things began to become clear.

'The next question, then, was this – how can a wasp be persuaded to hunt down and sting a particular person? For it seemed likely that Hugh Hembury would have been disposed of at his stables by the same method as carried off his brother Alistair in the landau. Well, a wasp, even a giant one, has the advantage of being compact enough to be delivered to its victim in a box. In Lord Alistair's case it was a cigar-box, a present, I dare say, from Mrs Partridge here. Hugh Hembury had also received a package. You may recall his brother telling us that he had been feeding the horses oatmeal biscuits at the time of his death. If we were to investigate I have no doubt we would find that those biscuits came in a tin, and that the tin was a present from Mrs Partridge.

'But even when successfully delivered, can the creature be depended upon to sting? The answer is, of course, that it cannot. You examined Hugh Hembury's body very thoroughly, Watson, and there was no doubt in your mind he died because his heart was transfixed by a rib-bone. And you were right. I am sure there were no stings on the man. The attempt to dispose of him had, in that sense, failed, because the insect had flown away. But before it managed to escape it aroused enough terror among the horses in that stable to provoke them into the stampede in which Mr Hembury was crushed to death. It was, you might say, a lucky break for the killer, and a very unfortunate one for Mr Hembury.

'And now, tonight, in this sweetbox, the last bee of all. I

wonder if it would have got Lady Hembury had we not been here? I think it might. It certainly seemed most determined.'

I turned to Cordelia. Her head was hung, but she had stood her ground bravely while she listened to Holmes' exposition. 'Why, Cordelia?' I asked, 'You've killed two people, and would have killed a third.'

'People, John?' she said, 'perhaps they are. But barely human beings. This woman and her family have worked such evil in this village. If you knew. . . .'

'About Jordan Farway and the hunting party?' said Holmes.

'Yes, Mr Holmes.' It was James Partridge who spoke now. 'But what perhaps you did not know is that *I* was in that hunting party. They were clever enough to recruit myself and a policeman and other "pillars of the community" to safeguard them from the consequences of their actions. Ever since that bloody day, Cordelia and I have been cajoled and threatened and blackmailed by Lady Hembury and her brood. We have had to do her bidding without argument all these years.'

'But James knew nothing about these deaths,' said Cordelia adamantly.

'No,' Holmes replied, 'you had time to deal with the candle balloon and the clockwork organ on your way to your evenings meetings with Lady Hembury.'

'And what was the point of all that, Cordelia?' I asked.

'I wanted them to suffer what Jordan Farway suffered when he heard that hunting horn. I wanted them to know the ineluctable approach of a dreadful death, to cringe in fear of it, powerless to stop its advance. I wanted them to experience the sheer terror of being hunted to death. And I am quite satisfied that they did. Now you had better arrest me.' She turned to her husband with a heart-breaking look of longing.

'James, my dear, what can I say? I despaired of ever escaping from their grip – or ever getting justice. I did hope at first I would not be found out, but when Mr Holmes and John came to stay I considered that if it were the will of God that I should be caught, then I would take my punishment.'

There was a moment of sorrowful silence as Holmes and I contemplated the unhappy couple. Lady Hembury, who had listened to everything in trembling confusion, seemed hardly able to comprehend any of it.

Then Holmes said, 'You might have escaped tonight, Mrs Partridge. Instead you came here to the Hall because you feared that Watson and myself might be in danger. That was a brave and generous act.

'I suggest, Reverend Partridge, that you and your wife go directly to your cottage and prepare yourself for a journey. For a long journey, somewhere far away.'

'Mr Holmes,' said Partridge, 'are you suggesting ... ?'

'Watson and I must find an inn for the night,' Holmes continued, 'and if, by, let us say, noon tomorrow, you have not left your cottage for some remote destination, we shall assume you would prefer to accompany us back to London.'

'Thank you, Mr Holmes,' said Cordelia, 'and thank you, John.' She took her husband's arm and, ignoring his surprise, led him, briskly out of the room.

Lady Hembury stirred from her trance. 'Where are they going?' she asked.

'A long way off,' said Holmes blandly, 'where the evil in this village can no longer touch them.'

'But she did not ask my permission. I gave her no instruction to leave. Call her back at once.'

'Goodnight, Lady Hembury,' said Holmes, leading me out.

'She had better be here tomorrow as usual,' called the old woman, 'or there'll be hell to pay. I am the Lady of the Manor. I am a Hembury. I am Lady Maude Hembury. Do you hear me sir?'

And we did, but only just, for by that time we were well down the corridor and almost to the front door.

The next morning the Partridge's cottage was empty. They had gone, and I have never seen either of them since. I know not whether they are happy or unhappy, home or abroad, comfortable or destitute, and I no longer expect to find out. Yet, in concert, I think, with all the villagers of Windwhistle, when I reflect with gratitude and relief that Hembury Hall is (since her ladyship's recent death) now empty of tyrants, I offer up a quiet petition of mercy for Cordelia Partridge, wherever she might be.

5

THE DEVIL'S TUNNEL

In the winter of 1882 during the early days with Sherlock Holmes at Baker Street, the strains of some rather irksome study I had taken up in the field of medicine had aroused in me a craving for lightweight entertainments. In particular I had taken a liking to those musical shows which specialize in tumblers, jugglers, and similar exotic displays, and which, for one or two sparkling hours, enabled me to forget the wearying concerns of my daily routine.

It was at the theatre that I was introduced by McKenna, a mutual friend, to Miss Sara Thackeray. As well as being an exceptionally beautiful woman, Miss Thackeray was a gifted stage performer. The daughter of Jonas Thackeray, the famous conjurer and magician, now dead, she was billed as:

THE DEMON'S DAUGHTER
THE TALENTED AND ALLURING
MISS SARA THACKERAY
Magician, Actress, Singer, Dancer
AND STAGE ILLUSIONIST *PAR EXCELLENCE*
ONLY HEIRESS OF THE FORMIDABLE MAGICAL
GENIUS OF HER FAMOUS LATE FATHER
JONAS 'MEPHISTO' THACKERAY

Her act was truly a *tour de force*. In the twenty minutes or so during which she held the stage, one had the impression less of watching a conjurer than of being present at a ceremony of true magic. The voluptuous fall of her voice, the direct and fearless way she had of engaging the audience and the fluid beauty of her physical movement all contrived to weave a spell which held the auditorium in a breathless hush. As the curtain fell upon her last trick, rapt silence would explode into an uninhibited roar of appreciation.

McKenna and I watched her performances over three consecutive evenings and, for the last, a Monday, he arranged for the three of us to dine together at Courtnay's just off the Strand. In the event, McKenna went down with influenza on the Sunday, but prevailed upon me to keep the appointment, with the happy result that I found myself looking forward to an evening upon which Miss Thackeray and I should dine together alone.

Still a single man, I had, perhaps, yet to outgrow that exquisite youthful susceptibility which makes any contact with a beautiful woman a likely occasion of enchantment. Since this was not a condition I wished to confide in my companion Sherlock Holmes, I had said nothing of my ensuing appointment when, late in the afternoon of that Monday, we sat together reading and smoking in our Baker Street sittingroom.

Suddenly, Holmes, who had been intermittently reading, puffing upon a pipeful of tobacco and taking swigs from a whisky glass, snapped his book shut and said, 'Watson, my friend, I have a surprise for you.'

'For me?' I put down my newspaper.

'We do not see enough of each other these days. I have been too long tied up with this tedious business of the railway parcel thefts, and you have been out every evening except Sunday for the last week. Tonight, therefore, I am going to treat you to an evening at the opera.'

'I say, that's very kind.'

'They are doing *Tannhauser* at Her Majesty's. I know how you like your Wagner, and this version is in English. I managed to acquire two box tickets for this evening and am certain it will prove the perfect fantasy for a gloomy winter night.'

'Did you say for this evening?'

'I have booked a cab to pick us up from here at seven. You will have plenty of time to wash and change.'

'Holmes – I'm terribly sorry. I wish you had given me fore-warning. I'm afraid I have an existing engagement.'

My colleague graciously endeavoured to conceal his dis-appointment. 'Oh. Well, no matter, I shall go alone. Your assig-nation is in London?'

'In the Strand,' I said cagily.

'You went to the Strand on Saturday evening.'

'I did.'

'And on Friday?'

'Yes, Holmes,' I said, resigning myself to a full confession, 'and, as a matter of fact on several other days. The fact is I have become friends with a certain lady of the theatre and we are meeting for dinner after her show.'

'Oh. May I ask which show?'

The paper I had been perusing, which was actually a few days old, lay open at a page carrying a short review of the entertainment in which Sara was playing. This I passed to Hol-mes who proceeded to read from it aloud.

'The evening provided excellent entertainment in a variety of styles, but nothing came quite so close to perfection as the astounding performance of Miss Sara Thackeray, enticingly billed as The Demon's Daughter. *The soubriquet is partly an* homage *to her late father, Jonas 'Mephisto' Thackeray, but also alerts us to the incendiary nature of a quite exceptional display of stage magic, in which a lot of smoke and red lighting add spectacularly to the illusion of diabolical influences. Miss Thackeray herself, dressed entirely in black, is always fetching and often mystifying, in an entertainment which is thoroughly and compulsively enjoyable.'*

Having finished reading aloud, Holmes then scanned the article again, silently, before handing it back to me.

'I can see,' he said, 'why *Tannhauser* might seem tame by

comparison. Well, you must certainly not let the good lady down, Watson. She is pretty, then?'

'Very pretty. But she is hardly more than an acquaintance and you are not to read blood-racing romance into the thing.'

'Really, Watson,' said Holmes impishly, 'to imagine I would suspect you of such impetuosity.'

It seemed to me that Sara's performance that night was better than ever. After the show we strolled out along the Strand where city lights blazed in the frosty February air. Courtnay's restaurant is off the south side of the Strand in one of those small dark streets that slope towards Victoria Embankment. While its exterior appearance is a little unprepossessing, it is quite charming inside, comfortable in a sedate sort of way, and not at all showy. It had not occurred to me that anyone could take exception to it, until, after we had settled at our table, I asked Sara for her opinion, expecting her merely to confirm the appropriateness of my choice.

'Well, John, it is pleasant here. And very quiet.'

'Come along. You are holding something back.'

'You're quite right,' said she, 'if we're going to get to know one another, there's no point wasting time with polite fictions. Well then, to be frank, I do find it a mite stuffy.'

'Stuffy?' I laughed. 'Sara, I fear you are too wild a creature for a steady fellow like myself.'

'There is nothing wrong in being steady. It is what I like about you, John, what makes me feel I can trust you.' She leaned closer, 'It is why I am going to ask you to help me.' Her smile had gone now and her brow knitted. 'It's to do with the two old aunts I live with – it's dreadful, John, it really is.'

'Tell me, Sara,' I said, 'I am listening.'

She then went on to tell me how, on the death of Jonas Thackeray, her father (her mother being already long dead) she had moved in with the two aunts, her father's maiden sisters. Their own father, Abram Thackeray, had been a stage magician himself, and their early lives had been blighted by poverty and unhappiness. But Abram finally made his fortune as an entertainer and when, on his death, the family inherited his money, all seemed to have worked out for the best. Jonas, however, took up his own father's mantle, going on to achieve a degree of celebrity as 'The Great Mephisto'. The effect of this was to resurrect the embarrassment of his sisters, for while enjoying their inherited wealth, they remained ashamed of its source, and determined that Sara herself should have nothing to do with the theatrical life.

As sole trustees of the family money, they warned her in no uncertain terms that, should she disobey them, she would inherit nothing. Since, however, the aunts never went out or received visitors and seldom read a newspaper, Sara decided that it would not be difficult for her to continue her career in secret. She told the old women that she was employed as companion to a Lady Rachel Eliot. On one occasion she had even taken them to tea at the Café Royal to meet this Lady Eliot, impersonated by an actress friend with such success that her aunts had commended her heartily upon acquiring a post with so elegant and accomplished a lady.

I chuckled greatly at this story, but poor Sara was not laughing.

'John, they've found out everything.'

'What?'

'There was a newspaper article on Saturday. . . .'

'A marvellous review. I saw it.'

'So, more's the pity, did they. A copy of the article came through the letterbox this morning addressed to Aunt Pem.'

'But who would wish to expose you in that way?'

'It's not important who. The thing is they now know that I have deceived them – that I never was the companion of any Lady Eliot and that, in defiance of their command, I have been working in the theatre for well over a year, and what's worse, as a magician. In short, I could not have made more certain of their anger had I conducted black masses in their sittingroom. They've cut me out of their wills. I may still live with them but after they are dead the money will go to charity.'

'Can they do this?'

'I'm afraid they can. My father was a fool about money and allowed the old biddies to control everything.'

'And will nothing change their minds?'

'Well,' she said, 'there is one possibility, but. . . .'

'But?'

'John, you and I hardly know one another. I don't wish to presume upon your kindness. It is a lot to ask.'

'Ask it, please. If I can help in any way it will be an honour and a delight.'

'Very well. Would you be prepared to make a railway journey with me?'

She then went on to outline her plan for getting back into her aunts' favours. Apparently the dangers of the wide world, and in particular an incident in which their trunk had been stolen from the luggage van of their train during a journey, had put them in mortal fear of travelling. As a result, the family home in Yorkshire had not been visited in two years, and they missed it terribly. Sara hoped that by offering to accompany them, and by supplying a trustworthy gentleman bodyguard to escort them upon the journey, she would win back their indebtedness and esteem. Being a physician, I was considered ideal for the role, for elderly ladies tend to put a lot of trust in medical men. All I would have to do would be to travel up with the Thackeray women to Yorkshire, stay overnight in the family house, and return to London on the following day. It seemed a simple enough request and I readily agreed. Sara was overjoyed.

As I ascended the stairs to our sittingroom in Baker Street an hour later, everything was so still that I imagined at first either that Holmes had stayed out after the opera, or was already in bed. Entering, however, I saw that my friend was stretched out, eyes closed, in one of the comfortable chairs next to the fire. I pushed the door quietly shut behind me.

'Good evening, Watson.'

'Holmes! I thought you were asleep.'

'I was ruminating. Do you know this book?'

He tossed me a small, board-bound volume which I opened at the title page: *Branch Lines – by James Henry Strachan – being a miscellany of facts, stories and anecdotes of the English railways*.

'I didn't know you were interested in such things, Holmes.'

'Oh it is fascinating stuff. But I had a particular reason to read it. You recall my mentioning the business of the parcel thefts on the South-East and Chatham railway? Well this little volume, with its thoroughness of detail, has enabled me to deduce how the thieves were able to spirit away an entire wagon, using a disused line as their bolt-hole.'

'Extraordinary,' I said blandly, not wanting to discuss railways, or my proposed journey, at that moment.

'I like trains, Watson. I find a railway journey relaxing, meditative. One can think on a train, don't you find?'

'Possibly,' I said in a mumbling sort of way, before wrestling to change the subject. 'How was the opera?'

'*Tannhauser*? You would have enjoyed it. A man is bewitched by a young woman who lures him to a magical mountain world. Of course, it all ends in disaster. How was your evening?'

'Oh, very good, really.'

'And Miss Sara Thackeray?'

'Is well.'

'Good. I see that her show is to run another week.'

'Yes.'

'And then Miss Thackeray moves on to other things?'

'She is taking a short holiday in Yorkshire.'

'Yorkshire. A bleak place at this time of year.'

'Yes. She is going up with her aunts, who are elderly.'

'You will miss her, I expect.'

Yet again, Holmes seemed to have brought me to an impasse where I must either tell everything or tell a lie. With a sigh I said, 'Actually, Holmes, I'm going with them.' I explained the entire business – the disinheritance, Sara's plan to recover it, and the rest.

'It is interesting,' said Holmes at the end of it all, 'that you are going to that particular part of Yorkshire. Your journey will take you through a legendary tunnel. I was reading about it just now in this book. Here.'

He found the place for me, where I read the following:

'The line to Quickfall on Strawberry Moor passes through the famous bore under Quickfall Edge known

*locally as "The Devil's Tunnel". Legend has it that this
tunnel is haunted by the spirit of Lord Wilfred George
Harewood, the so-called "Hanging Judge" who, in
October 1878, travelling from London to his Yorkshire
home, was alive and laughing when his train entered
the tunnel, but stone dead of a stroke when it emerged
from the other end. The story went that the Devil had
"collected" the judge's spirit on its passage through that
grim tunnel, and that it remains to this day a sort of
diabolical man-trap for lost souls.'*

'What do you think?' asked Holmes with a challenging grin.

'Fanciful,' I said, 'but a rather good yarn.'

'It sounds to me,' replied my friend, 'that it is a thoroughly
bewitching mountain world you are being lured into.'

It was a full week before I joined Sara Thackeray and her
aunts Pem and Ruth on the train from London. The two
elderly women were formidable characters. Ruth was plump
and rotund, well-mannered but unsmiling. Her clothes
showed some remnants of a certain gaiety of spirit – a small
flash of orange in the fabric of her otherwise brown dress, and
a pretty jewelled pendant on a chain round her neck.

Pem, however, was the very incarnation of austerity. She
was small and, probably, thin and bony, though the copious
folds of black taffeta that made up her garment hid the shape
of her limbs entirely and a black veil descending from under
her velvet hat concealed even the shape of her features. She
had, according to Sara, been severely scarred by smallpox
during her miserable childhood, and never showed her face to
strangers. A pair of sharp eyes peered out through the veil,
surrounded by skin of apparently exceptional whiteness.

Sara's own outfit was remarkably like Pem's in style, fabric
and general effect, though on Sara it looked positively
fetching. I felt certain this coincidence of fashion was not fortuitous, but another of Sara's shameless attempts to win over
the old lady.

The first part of our journey went reasonably smoothly,

though the aunts, while expressing gratitude for my company, clearly suspected my credentials as a genuine doctor. Having been once fooled by Sara, they were not to be easily convinced that I was not just some audacious thespian impersonating a medic for Sara's long-term ends. They asked me all sorts of details about my qualifications, even about specific diseases and conditions. At first, they drank in all the anatomical minutiae I could oblige them with, but it was not long before they wearied of this grim diversion. I was glad to have the excuse of rushing off along the corridor to the luggage van every ten minutes to check that their trunk was still there.

When we changed, some hours later, onto the branch-line that was to take us into Yorkshire, our journey became rather uncomfortable. The train had no corridor, and luggage was carried in a separate wagon. Because the theft the ladies had experienced some years before had been from this very train and Pem was somewhat agitated about it, she had instructed Sara to arrange in advance that we should remain with the trunk for the rest of our journey, even though this meant travelling in the luggage wagon. The irony of the situation was that it was Pem herself who complained loudest about the conditions in which we now found ourselves.

Being large, drafty and relatively empty, the luggage wagon was colder than the compartment in which we had travelled up from London. There was one exterior door on either side of the carriage, but none connecting it to other carriages. The only seats were two small stools which folded down from the wagon wall, and these were taken by the two aunts, while Sara and I perched ourselves on items of luggage, she on a packing case between the old ladies, I on a suitcase facing them. The trunk was a very large, black boxwood affair, inlaid with patches of Turkish carpet. It was so colossally heavy that the porters who manhandled it into the wagon had left it as near to the door as possible.

The legend of the Devil's Tunnel, through which our branch-line journey was soon to take us, was well known to the aunts. Aunt Pem even remembered meeting the fated hanging Judge once when she was a child. And while plump, sensible Aunt Ruth poo-pooed the gruesome stories as fanciful nonsense, Pem was clearly a little disturbed by them. She expressed the desire to be 'through the other side of the confounded tunnel and on the way to Strawberry Moor' just as soon as possible.

I was, I admit, looking forward to the end of the journey myself. The aunts and I had run out of conversation and, in their company, Sara and I could talk only trivialities. I contented myself with watching the bleak, winter moorland roll past the carriage window. Then Sara shouted out, with an excited laugh, 'Here we are, John. Quickfall Edge. Almost to the terrible tunnel!' The embankments were rising in the direction of the train, gradually at first, then all at once in a surge. Suddenly, with a colossal roar, we were inside the tunnel. Thrown into the total darkness of the unlit wagon, we were so deafened by the noise that we could not hear one another at all except at a shout.

'It's too dark,' Aunt Pem whimpered from her seat opposite me.

'Never mind, I've got your hand,' Sara shouted back.

'It's the noise I can't abide,' said Aunt Ruth.

'A few minutes and we'll be out,' yelled Sara cheerily, heartily playing the part of the doting niece.

It was at this moment that the first singular thing happened. Suddenly there came a shriek from the seat opposite me.

'Aunt Pem – what is it?'

'My arm. Something scratched my arm.'

'You must have snagged yourself,' I heard Ruth say, 'on a pin in your dress.'

'I have no pins in my dress. A pin in *your* dress, perhaps, Ruth. Heavens, I am so hot. Please – will somebody open the window?'

'I will do it if you wish,' I yelled, 'but I fear we'll let in a lot of smoke and steam.'

'It doesn't matter. I must have air,' replied the old woman anxiously, 'Please, Doctor Watson, if you would be so kind.'

I groped my way to the door, found the catch, and let down the window. The noise became even louder. Smoke, grit and steam whirled into the compartment. Feeling my way back to my seat I heard Sara consoling her troubled old aunt.

'There. Let me put my arm round you.'

'Thank you, Sara, dear. You are a comfort, you really are.'

For several minutes we endured the maelstrom of noise and repellent odours. Then I heard Sara's voice again, lifted above the racket.

'How are you holding out, dear Aunt Pem?'.

'I am gritting my teeth and hating every passing second.'

'Aunt Ruth?'

'I shall survive. I have been passing the minutes imagining us all taking a cream tea in the music room at Strawberry House. I take it you still like cream teas, Sara?'

Sara did not answer, and Aunt Pem put in, even louder, 'I don't think you heard what Ruth asked you, dear. Cream teas. Do you still like them?'

A pause, then, 'Sara? Sara, are you all right?'

And at that moment the train left the tunnel for blinding daylight, revealing in an instant an appalling reality – there were only three of us in the wagon. Sara Thackeray was gone.

Ruth began screaming. I rushed toward the open window, leading out to look back along the track, but between the train and the receding tunnel mouth there was nothing to be seen.

'Doctor Watson,' Aunt Ruth called to me frantically, 'stop the train!'

I pulled the emergency handle and the train stopped.

It is a day I would not live through again for all the gold in Africa, torn as I was between my duty to two distraught elderly women and my own grief and confusion at Sara's disappearance.

It fell to me to take some sort of charge over the business of establishing a search, in which one Cedric Hayes, a local policeman, proved willing but lamentably inexperienced. We scoured every nook and cranny of the train several times over. We had the tunnel gone over in both directions with torches. We were rewarded, if that is the right word, with two finds. One of Sara's shoes lay at the mouth of the tunnel and, some way in, her hat. But there was no trace of a body. We could only surmize that she had either fallen or jumped from the train and had not been killed outright but, probably dreadfully injured, had dragged herself out of the tunnel. But even if this extraordinary hypothesis were right, where was she now?

I asked Hayes to send a wire from his police station requesting Holmes to come to Yorkshire immediately. A local man then drove the two aunts to their home on Strawberry Moor and I went on to the village of Quickfall where I put up at the Pilgrim's Arms, securing Holmes a room at the same time. After that I lay on the bed and fell into a tortured sleep, dreaming terrible dreams.

When I awoke, it was early evening and already dark. Downstairs in the tavern I could hear the talk and laughter of a few early patrons. The fire that had been lit for me in my room before I fell asleep had now burned down to smouldering ash, and I was cold. I tidied myself up and descended to the saloon bar, where I sat in a corner with a glass of whisky and water. Some details of Sara's disappearance had now reached the village and were naturally the subject of much speculation. I refrained from identifying myself, fearing I might be badgered for details I had no wish to supply. It was in this lonely and miserable frame of mind that I eventually looked up to see a tall, thin, silhouette pass the window and step towards the door of the bar. Holmes had arrived.

He had left London for Yorkshire the moment he received my telegram. Now as we sat together in the bar, the effects of several whiskies and my delight in seeing him temporarily inured me to the worst of my sorrow. Holmes questioned me about every detail of the journey.

Afterwards he said, 'It is an exceptional case, Watson, for you were there when this remarkable thing happened – an "eye" witness, only, of course, the darkness made you a completely blind one. So, let me recapitulate: the train enters the tunnel; Sara Thackeray's Aunt Pem complains of a sharp, stabbing sensation. When she becomes hot, you open the carriage window. The last time you hear Sara Thackeray speak is only moments before the train emerges from the tunnel? How many moments?'

'Fifteen or twenty seconds, I should say.'

'And in that twenty seconds, Miss Thackeray seems to have vanished into thin air.'

'The poor, dear, girl,' I said, as the grief suddenly returned to me in a sharp pang.

'You are right, I would say,' continued Holmes, 'to speculate that her chances of surviving a fall from the train would be remote. I observed on my journey here that the tunnel bore is not much larger than the train. A person falling or jumping from the window would surely be shattered against the tunnel wall.' Then he seemed to light upon an idea. 'How are the two aunts?'

'Miss Ruth remained in control of herself. Miss Pem was quite hysterical. They are at their house on Strawberry Moor. I must say they seem genuinely upset, however badly they may have treated the girl before.'

'Well, then, my dear friend, let us find some transport and get out to Strawberry Moor immediately.'

Strawberry House was a rambling dwelling of cold, grey stone. From the narrow highway, a barely driveable track of shale and ash led us the last, dark quarter mile to the front door, the wind dogging us with cold blasts as we approached.

It was Ruth Thackeray who showed us in, her sister Pem having taken to her bed upon arrival, apparently thrown into severe shock as a result of the trials of the day.

With the house in virtual disuse for two years, only one servant had been retained to keep the place in tolerable order, a local man by the name of Braithwaite who, apart from his ongoing duties in their absence, acted as housekeeper, butler and parlourmaid whenever the old ladies were in residence. It was Braithwaite who brought us tea and stacked up the fireplace as Holmes began to question Ruth Thackeray about her missing niece. He repeated all the questions he had previously put to me, confirming the order and timing of the incidents upon the train that day, before he began to probe more deeply into the family history.

'I gather from Doctor Watson that your relationship with your niece Sara was not always a happy one.'

Miss Thackeray's eyes hardened. 'From the day the girl's father died and she came to live with us we found her rebellious, self-willed and lawless. Even though she knew how my sister Pem abhorred everything to do with the theatrical profession, she was determined to become a common playhouse libertine. That is no life for a decent woman.'

Holmes stroked his chin thoughtfully and said, 'I think, Miss Thackeray, it is time for us to talk to your sister.'

'Out of the question, Mr Holmes. She's in no state to talk to anyone. I fear her mind is a little gone. She has started to have ludicrous fancies – about devils and the like.'

Holmes, however, was adamant. 'Should your niece Sara be found dead, the police may choose to instigate a murder enquiry. In that event, the passengers who shared that railway wagon will be the most obvious suspects. Now, I would be grateful if you would show us directly to your sister's room.'

I cannot recall a gloomier atmosphere than that which prevailed in Miss Pem Thackeray's bedroom. The thick curtains, drawn shut, permitted hardly any daylight, and the fabrics and hangings, in faded burgundies and mauves, told a story of days of splendour now lost in memory. Though I had no reason to doubt Sara's declaration that the aunts were keepers of a sizeable fortune, they were clearly not inclined to spend much of it upon the commonplaces of everyday living.

To one side stood a huge and ugly four-poster bed, canopied in the same heavy fabric as the shrouded windows. The curtains at the visible side of the bed were pulled across, leaving only a slight gap through which could dimly be seen a wizened-looking, nightcapped head. Miss Ruth Thackeray bade Holmes and myself move a couple of chairs to the bedside, while she herself, standing, leaned over to rouse her sister.

'Pem. It's Ruth. Can you hear me?'

There was a slight stirring within the canopied enclosure.

'Do you remember,' continued Miss Thackeray, 'Doctor Watson who came up with us from London?'

'Doctor London?' asked a creaky old voice.

'Doctor Watson. Sara's friend.'

'Oh him. Yes,' said the voice within.

'He has come to see you. With his colleague, Mr Sherlock Holmes. They are trying to find out what happened to Sara.'

A hand inside the huge tent of fabric moved the curtain a little bit aside and the occupant was revealed a little. In fact, I could see more of Pem Thackeray now than I had earlier that day on the train journey, for although her nightcap was tight around her forehead, her eyes were more clearly visible, showing the pallid skin of old age, its deep scars the familiar legacy of a childhood smallpox. All other detail was lost in the gloom.

'We know what happened to Sara,' said the hard little voice, 'she was taken.'

Holmes edged closer on his chair. 'Taken, Miss Thackeray?'

'She should have heeded the Good Book. "Woe to women who sew magic charms."'

'You think she was abducted from the train by some supernatural force?'

'Body and soul. But that is not the end of it, sir.'

'Not the end? What do you mean, Miss Thackeray?' Holmes asked gently.

'Let the doctor come nearer,' said the voice.

I leaned across in front of Holmes so that I was within a mere twelve inches of the face in the curtained cavern, at which a thin hand was thrust at me, or, rather, a wrist, for the hand itself was concealed in a lace glove.

'Look at this,' said Miss Thackeray.

What I saw was a scratch-mark, quite superficial, which might have been made with the sharp end of a needle. There was nothing odd about it, except that it was in the form of a rough, unfinished 'S', but to Miss Thackeray, this seemed to be all-significant.

'It happened to me in that tunnel, Doctor. And I am no fool. I know what it means. I am marked. They will come for me next. Tonight, I dare say, or tomorrow. But I care not. Let them come. I shall go quietly. I have made my will and I am ready.'

At which point she hastily drew the curtains of the bed fully across the little opening, and disappeared within.

'Send them away, Ruth,' she called in a muffled voice, 'and tell them they are wasting their time. Sara is lost.'

When we had returned to the downstairs, Holmes put two last questions to Miss Ruth Thackeray.

'Your sister Pem mentioned that she has remade her will this day.'

'That is correct. She insisted, She has made over her own half of the estate to a charity which looks after impoverished children. She says she hopes by that to save at least a few young souls from the miseries of such a childhood as we knew ourselves.'

'Thank you, Miss Thackeray. And one last thing. The trunk in which you brought your possessions to Yorkshire today – is it unpacked?'

'Yes. Pem unpacked it herself soon after we arrived.'

'Your sister unpacked it?'

'Yes.'

'Then I wonder if I might borrow it. There is an experiment I should like to conduct. It may help us in our efforts to solve the mystery of your missing niece.'

'Then, Mr Holmes, take it, do. It is in the lumber-room. Braithwaite will show you where. He will help you with it to your transport.'

As we drove back across the moor, the large, ornate trunk in the back of our wagon, I said to Holmes, 'I'm afraid I cannot see how this thing will help us. It is quite empty.'

'Not quite, Watson,' replied my friend, 'You will notice that there is a grey, powdery deposit in the bottom. But you're right, of course. I'm not sure that it will help us at all. We are simply keeping all options open. Sara Thackeray definitely left that tunnel in some way or other – either in the train, out of it, or on top of it. If either of the latter, why was there no blood? At best she would have been seriously injured. Of course, the hat and shoe could have been thrown from the train as blinds. But if she was in the train, where was she?'

'Aha! I see what you are thinking. That she could have been in the trunk.'

'If what you have told me is true, Watson, how could that be possible? Is there not a problem of time? You have said that only a few seconds elapsed between Sara's last words and the moment the train emerged from the tunnel. Was it long enough for a person to have clambered into a trunk?'

'You're right, Holmes. Not nearly long enough. Besides, the trunk was full and colossally heavy. I helped carry it myself. And why should Sara want to connive her disappearance in such a mysterious way, when she might have simply run off?'

'Quite so.'

'Then what did happen?'

'Until I have concluded my experiment, I cannot be sure. We will know more tonight, after we have kept our last appointment.'

'But Holmes – at this hour? Everywhere is shut.'

'Oh no, my dear fellow. This is one place which is always open.'

This last remark turned out to be one of Holmes' jokes, for our destination was none other than the Devil's Tunnel itself. We drove there by way of Quickfall village, where we unloaded the trunk at the inn before borrowing lanterns and waterproofs. Long before we reached the Quickfall end of the tunnel, night had come down.

We retrod the ground my earlier search had covered, walking the entire length of the tunnel toward the end where the train had entered. It was a long trek and I was wet, exhausted and irritable as we approached the further opening.

'I don't see what we will find at this end, Holmes. As I told you, Sara spoke only seconds before the train left the tunnel. It is surely near the exit we should find clues. That was where we came upon the shoe and the hat.'

'You've noticed nothing of interest, then?'

'Nothing,' I said.

'It's underfoot you should be looking,' said my friend. 'This is the fifth we have come across.'

He pointed to a large, chalky boulder.

'The rock?' I said.

'They occur at intervals of about two hundred yards.'

'Fallen from the tunnel roof, I suppose.'

'How so? The roof is of brick.'

'So it is. But bits of stone – what on earth can they tell us?'

'Have you not noticed, Doctor, that they seem to be of the same, powdery grey stone which we found in the bottom of the trunk? I think that they may actually tell us a good deal. However, I shall spend the night giving the matter some proper thought. Come along. Let us get out of this dismal place and seek ourselves out a hot pie at the inn.'

After a late supper, which I was too exhausted to enjoy much, we retired to our rooms on the first floor. These were adjacent and overlooked the street and the deep, bubbling river that ran into Quickfall through a small threshing-mill.

Holmes was planning to stay up all night with his pipe, and had arranged for an adequate supply of logs to be brought to his room to sustain him through his vigil. It was a relief to me to leave everything in his capable hands while I refreshed myself with a much-needed night's sleep. But as I lay in that strange bed with the wind wuthering about the eaves of the inn in its lonely, wailing way, my thoughts turned again to Sara, and the unfathomable mystery of her sudden disappearance. It was probably two whole hours before I fell asleep.

A little before dawn, I found myself again awake. There was a commotion out in the street – the coughing of a horse, a man's voice calling out – then Holmes shouting back from the window of the room next door.

'You'd better tek 'er in, sir,' said the voice below, 'she's in a desperate way.'

'Very well,' Holmes was saying, 'bring her upstairs at once.'

My heart raced. Had Sara been found, then? And what did the fellow mean by a 'desperate' state? While I dressed, noises in the corridor outside my room told me that a distraught woman had been brought upstairs and taken into the small sittingroom which was part of the suite occupied by Holmes and myself. Then I heard Holmes ordering brandy and one of the inn's serving girls setting off downstairs to fetch it.

I hastily put a dressing-gown over my shirt and went into the corridor, hoping beyond hope that I might find Sara sitting in the room with Holmes. But as I crossed the threshold, my heart sank. It was not Sara Thackeray who lay there, reclining pale-faced upon the small settee, but her plump Aunt Ruth.

At first her state of shock caused her to tremble uncontrollably, and its effect upon her breathing meant that her words came in stuttered gasps. But as she told her story, her composure returned. The news was indeed extraordinary. It transpired that her sister Pem had that very night disappeared, under the strangest conditions, from Strawberry House.

'After making Pem a nightcap,' Ruth Thackeray told us, 'I retired to bed with a book, Braithwaite having returned earlier to his cottage across the yard. I suppose it was a little after midnight when I heard the first noise – a large, dull, thump, as though something had fallen on the floor in Pem's room. This was followed a little while after by another noise, as if some heavy object were being dragged across the floor. I should have run in then and seen what was up, but all Pem's talk of lost souls had made me jittery. Cowardice got the better of me and I persuaded myself it was only the wind I was hearing. However, when the noises persisted, I opened the window and called for Braithwaite, waving my lantern in the window in the hope of attracting his attention. But the wind was wild and with one breath blew away both my voice and the stuttering flame. Whatever lurked outside my room had begun by this time to drag and thump step by step down the long staircase. Certain now that these were no natural noises, I began to call and call until, at last, Braithwaite heard me and came running across to the house.

'Mr Holmes, Doctor Watson, when we went into Pem's room, there was no sign of her anywhere. She was not in the house, or in the yard, and we drove around the moor in the wagon before coming here but found not a trace. She has disappeared, and the devil knows where. My fear is,' and here she hesitated, as though finding the thought intolerable, 'my fear is that in her weakness of mind she has dragged herself out of the house and is now wandering about somewhere on the open moor in a delirium. If she is not already dead.'

While Ruth Thackeray was telling her story, Braithwaite made contact with the local vicar, who kindly agreed to put Miss Ruth Thackeray up until more was known about the peculiar events at Strawberry House. It was six-thirty in the morning before all this was settled and, with Holmes already abandoned to the idea of being up all night, I decided to join him for an early breakfast in the diningroom, though I had little appetite myself.

'Do you believe Pem Thackery might still be alive?' I asked.

'I fear not.'

'You will want to go out to Strawberry House again?'

'Yes, Watson. And then to Innsford, the next station up the line, so that we can take a train journey of our own through this Devil's Tunnel. That experiment I mentioned.'

I was about to ask more when there was, again, a build-up of noise outside the inn. On investigation we found that a crowd had gathered around the threshing-mill, where they were disentangling something large and black from the mill-wheel.

We made our way over. It was a dull, chill morning with the sun hardly up, and Mr Basham, the landlord of the Pilgrim's Arms, tall and black-bearded, was supervising activities.

'Well, Mr Holmes,' he said as we approached, 'thou'rt a detective. What does tha make o' this? It's old Miss Thackeray from Strawberry House. Looks like she fell in river upstream, drowned, and were carried down into millwheel. Look at 'er, though. Bent like a gatespring, this way and that.'

It was true. The body of Pem Thackeray was doubled up almost into an S-shape.

'Well,' said Holmes to me quietly, 'we are at least saved the inconvenience of a trip to Strawberry House.'

'You think there is nothing to be discovered there?'

'Oh, there will be signs and clues galore, I've no doubt. But we've more urgent business – just as soon as I've settled a few things.'

With this he embarked upon a private conversation with the Pilgrim's landlord, eventually accompanying that gentleman back into the inn. I returned to my room and waited there until

Holmes knocked at about eight o'clock, declaring that it was now time for us to make our way to Innsford station, where we would begin the trip which would settle everything.

The train from Innsford through the Devil's Tunnel and on to Quickfall would be the first of the day. While I waited on the platform, Holmes went off to do some business with the stationmaster and, a little later, to my amazement, emerged from the station office once again in the company of Mr Basham, the bearded publican from the Pilgrim's Arms. They were pushing a trolley upon which rested the large trunk which Holmes had acquired the day before from the Thackeray household.

'Mr Basham here,' said Holmes, 'has agreed to help us with our experiment. He will travel with us as far as Quickfall – in the luggage wagon.'

While the train hissed and steamed in the station, the three of us manhandled the heavy and cumbersome box into a wagon identical to that from which Sara Thackeray had disappeared on the previous afternoon. Then the train doors slammed, the whistle blew, and we were away.

'Well, Holmes,' I said, 'it is deuced heavy. What is in it? A brace of anvils, I should think.'

He laughed. 'Never mind that, now. We are approaching the tunnel and I wish, as far as possible, to reconstruct every detail of yesterday's events. As I recall your saying, you were facing the engine.'

'Yes. About here.'

'With the older Miss Thackerays opposite you, upon the folding seats, where Mr Basham is now?'

'That's right. And Sara about where you are, upon a packing-case.

'Excellent. Now, when the train enters the tunnel I should like you to do just as I ask. I promise everything will soon be clear. In the meantime, my dear fellow, you can comfort yourself with the certainty that Sara Thackeray was not killed. Neither did she run away.'

But I had hardly time to take in this last prodigious remark when darkness descended and, with a great scream of noise, we had entered the tunnel. A tremor of fear assailed me. Yesterday's awful events were still so vivid in my mind that I began very quickly to give way to irrational speculation. Suppose Holmes had made a mistake in his calculations? If there had been one inexplicable disappearance, why could there not be a second? What if there really were palpable evil lurking in this tunnel? But my companion now began to holler at me above the din.

'Think back, Watson. To yesterday. Sara, yourself and the two aunts. The train has just entered the tunnel. What now?'

'Pem complains of a scratching on her arm. She says she is hot and asks for the window to be opened. I grope my way in the darkness to the window, fumble for the strap and open it.'

'Do it, then, Watson, if you would.'

I complied. Noise roared in.

'You see what I mean, Holmes? About the smell? The din?'

'Just what she needed, Doctor, to carry out the plans without anyone noticing. Noise, darkness and a strong smell.'

'I don't follow. Just what *who* needed?'

'Sara Thackeray.'

'Sara?'

'She was speaking the truth when she told you she meant to regain her inheritance, Watson. But she never planned to do it by gentle persuasion. Her method was murder.'

'But she is the victim in this dreadful affair. How could she . . .?'

But my friend was not listening to my protestations.

'How much longer before we leave the tunnel, Doctor?'

'I cannot see to look at my watch, but I'd reckon about a minute.'

'We are coming close to that point, then, at which you last heard Sara Thackeray speak.'

'Yes. Some remark to her Aunt Ruth about the excitement of the holiday. Then idle chatter about cream teas, to which Sara did not reply, neither the first nor the second time she was asked. And with that, the train left the tunnel, and Sara was gone.'

At this moment, our own train whistled, the screech lingering like a death-wail in the tunnel confines. I was tired and confused. I wanted this all to be over.

'It's been a cold winter, Mr Basham,' said Holmes suddenly. It seemed to me an extraordinarily bland remark and I could only imagine my colleague had made it in order to introduce our hitherto silent fellow passenger into the conversation.

'It has that,' the publican replied, 'nowt but snow, ice and hard ground. There's not a farmer in Yorkshire won't be glad to see the first green of Spring.'

Deciding it would be ungracious not to participate in this small-talk I added, 'They are saying in London it is the worst winter for years. Are they not, Holmes?'

There was no reply. I assumed the noise had prevented my friends from hearing me. I said again, 'Aren't they, Holmes?'

Still there was no reply. An awful sense of dread descended upon me. I raised my voice and leaned forward, telling myself either he simply had not heard, or was just ignoring me.

'Holmes, I wish you would not play games with me. You should know that these last two days. . . .'

But I proceeded no further, for this was the moment at which the train left the tunnel, light filled the carriage, and I realized to my horror that Holmes was no longer with us.

'Mr Basham,' I called out to the black-bearded publican, who seemed to be quite unaware of what had happened, 'where is he?'

I rushed to the window, just as on the previous day, to peer back along the track. I would have pulled the emergency handle to stop the train except that my sense of *déjà-vu* was so overwhelming that by not pulling it I hoped to stave off an exact repeat of yesterday's nightmare.

Then I said, 'Good Lord, Basham, where in heaven's name can he have gone?' to which the man in the black beard replied, in Holmes unmistakable voice, 'I'm here, of course.'

'Holmes! It's you. In a false beard. And that fellow's jacket. But then – where is *he*?'

'In here,' said my friend calmly, pointing to the trunk. 'Where else could he be?'

He tapped on the trunk and it opened. There inside was Basham, down on his haunches, his chest on his knees, in a sort of S-shape.

He uncurled and stepped out onto the floor.

'Thank you, Mr Basham,' said Holmes, 'I wanted to make sure it could be done in the time available and, of course, it could. Plenty of time for Sara to accomplish everything she needed to.'

'Accomplish what?' said I.

'Oh Watson, isn't it clear to you yet? Sara had planned the whole business. When the train entered the tunnel, her first task was to dispose of her Aunt Pem. This she did with a needle tainted with a lethal poison. A scratch was enough, and the smell of the tunnel adequately disguised the odour of the chemical as it began to spread. The noise, meanwhile, masked the next part of the plan, to remove from the trunk the rocks with which she had weighted it, and hurl them from the window.'

'Those rocks we found at regular intervals when we searched the tunnel.'

'Precisely. Because she knew that when the trunk left the train it would be seven stones heavy, the weight of the dead body of Pem Thackeray. After poisoning her aunt, Sara packed her body into the trunk, neatly folded, just like Mr Basham here. Once rigor-mortis set in, the body became stiffened in that strange position – hence the S-shaped corpse this morning at the mill-wheel.'

'You mean the body found at the mill had not drowned?'

'Pem Thackeray was long dead when her body was ditched in the river last night.'

'But we talked to Pem Thackeray yesterday at Strawberry House. How could she have died on that train?'

'It was not Pem Thackeray in that bed, Watson. It was Sara. She had first adopted the disguise here on the train in the darkness, in the same way that I, just now, metamorphosed into Mr Basham here. As you noted, her outfit was quite

similar to her aunt's, and only needed a couple of additions –
the veil and the black lace rose, to make the transformation
complete. In the bedroom, of course, stage make-up had been
added to improve the illusion, creating those pock-marks and
other subtle details.'

'Yet they were conversing, here on this train, right to the last
second – both Sara and her Aunt Pem.'

'Watson – Sara Thackeray is an actress. Easy for her to hold
a conversation with herself, using both Pem's voice and her
own, long after the old lady was packed away dead in that
trunk.'

'Then the business last night at Strawberry House – the
noises that Ruth Thackeray heard. . . .'

'Well, just think. There was Sara in bed, disguised as her
Aunt Pem, with the dead body of the real Pem Thackeray
stashed away in some cupboard. The body had to be disposed
of, and those thumping noises were made by Sara dragging
the corpse downstairs and away to the river, from where, in
due course, it was washed down to Quickfall Mill. All that
nonsense so-called "Pem" spoke in her delirium to us yesterday – about being taken away – was intended to put us into the
frame of mind to accept the discovery of Pem's body as a mis-
adventure, or suicide.'

I could only succumb to the logic of Holmes' exposition.

'So where is Sara now?' I asked.

'We'll find her, Watson. The new will which "Pem" Thackeray made yesterday to this children's charity – I have no
doubt we will find the only beneficiary to be none other than
Sara Thackeray herself.

A change in the rhythm of the engine told us that the train
had begun to slow down on its approach to Quickfall station.
Then, just as it was stopping, something caught Holmes' eye
on the opposite platform. A young man in a tweed suit and
spectacles was standing there, waiting for the London train,
which was even then approaching.

Suddenly Holmes yelled, 'Good Lord! Quick! Excuse us, Mr
Basham!' and leaping from our carriage before the train had
quite stopped, still wearing his false black beard, he went

dashing off up the platform to cross the line by the bridge. Baffled, I followed after at a slower trot.

The younger man on the opposite platform, presumably under the impression that we were running for the train, hardly noticed us until we were upon him.

'Miss Thackeray!' said Holmes.

The young man turned, his face suddenly pale. And then I saw that it was indeed Sara, her hair pushed into a tweed cap, a pair of wire-framed spectacles on her nose.

She did not try to run, nor to remonstrate with us. She saw at once that it was all over for her.

'No point in pretending any more, Sara,' I said, 'Mr Holmes knows everything.'

'A fairly clever disguise,' said Holmes, 'and had it not been so early in the morning, you would no doubt have got away to London. But from our vantage point over there, with the sun behind us, while I could see reflections from the waitingroom windows, there was none from your spectacles. Obviously there is no glass in them. Besides, young men who wear tweed suits and hats of this outmoded sort are rarely so fashion-conscious as to ensure that their shoes, and luggage complement one another so artistically. I fear it was your good taste that gave you away.'

'Oh Lord,' she said, quietly. 'John, I deceived you.'

'Yes, you did.'

'I'm sorry.'

'Are you?'

'Yes. Really sorry.'

'Odd to think,' I said, 'that when I thought I was examining your Aunt Pem's arm last evening, it was actually you I was touching.'

'It was hard for me too,' she said with all the conviction in the world. 'How I wanted you to go on holding me.'

'I don't think,' I said sadly, 'that I would ever again believe any word you ever said to me, Miss Thackeray, however sincerely you spoke it.'

'Well,' she replied coolly, 'you know us theatre people, John. Make-believe is our business.'

6

THE HORROR OF HANGING WOOD

One bitterly cold March morning while London was still in darkness, a knock on the door of my room at our lodging house in Baker Street woke me with a start. Sherlock Holmes, not by nature an early riser, put his head around the door of my room to inform me that a carriage awaited us below in the street, that I should dress directly in winter clothes and that I must dismiss any thought of breakfast, for a journey had to be made immediately.

I complied hurriedly with my friend's request, though the room was cold and the darkness outside forbidding, for I detected in his tone that urgency which I know from long experience will be neither denied nor forestalled. Within ten minutes we were closing the front door of the lodging house and stepping onto a pavement whited by frost, where a four-wheeler awaited us. The driver sat up top, puffing fog through his muffler, and within the carriage, also huddled against the cold, there was a passenger.

'Lestrade,' I said, recognizing the grim face of the Inspector from Scotland Yard, 'so it was you who knocked us up.'

'My apologies, Doctor Watson. Do get in, please, and let's shut the door. It's deuced cold.'

Even with the windows fast shut and the three of us huddled together, the carriage got little warmer.

'And where on earth,' I enquired, 'might you be taking us at this hour?'

'To a nice little spot near Charlton village, Doctor.'

'A long, cold drive, then.'

'If you think it is cold now, you should have been there at four o'clock this morning.'

'No doubt. But what took you there at such an hour?'

'You'll see, Doctor, in good time.'

'Lestrade,' said Holmes, who had evidently spoken with the policeman before I emerged from my room, 'refuses to be drawn upon the matter. He is keen to preserve our judgement from any prejudice, so that we might come fresh to the facts.'

'It is one of those affairs,' said Lestrade, 'with the sort of meretritious surface features which might distract an investigator from pursuing the obvious line of enquiry, whereas I am convinced it is basically a very simple matter.' And, for the remainder of the journey, that was as far as he would be drawn.

Our journey took us just outside Charlton to a forested shallow valley known in the district as Hanging Wood. We were still more than an hour from dawn, but the sky was clear and a good spill of light from a three-quarter moon enabled us at least to distinguish the trees from the spaces between them.

The four-wheeler, having travelled as far as possible along a narrow track into the woods, stopped in a small clearing. From there, after we had been issued with lanterns, Holmes and I followed Lestrade into the trees. As we went deeper, the white fires of other lanterns winked at us through the dark thickets. The forest was, it seemed, already buzzing with police activity.

We stopped beside a ditch in which the shallow black water had turned to ice. Half in and half out of the ditch, a tarpaulin had been drawn over a man-shaped heap.

'This is what you brought us to see?' said Holmes.

'Yes, Holmes. This fellow was killed some time during the night. A robbery, I am sure.'

He drew back the tarpaulin. It was an ugly sight. The man's face had been battered out of all recognition, the nose crushed deep into the face. It appeared that the jaw had been shattered too, so that the upper teeth had skewed around almost ninety degrees from normal, giving the mouth the look of having twisted sideways. The man's black overcoat and the cheap suit beneath it were both torn. There was blood upon them, and one other terrible injury. The left arm had been broken at the shoulder with such ferocity that it was virtually detached from the body. As I lowered my lantern I could see through the tear in the man's shirt that only a few bloody threads of ligament and muscle maintained its connection to the torso.

'If it was robbery,' said Holmes, 'it was a brutal one.'

'Well, I dare say the chap resisted,' said Lestrade, 'and there are some nasty characters about, as you know, who like their demands to be complied with unerringly. Which is why I've asked you here, really. You know the methods of more of London's villains than any of us, both through personal encounter and your extensive studies. I want you to identify the author of this gruesome bit of handiwork, or at least provide me with a couple of possible names to add to my list.'

Holmes bent down to examine the wrecked body. It was, it seemed to me, an action designed to give him time to consider Lestrade's request. Eventually he looked up at the Inspector.

'I am not certain why you think this man was robbed.'

'Well, he has nothing of value on him. No wallet, no change. You will have noted the tear in his waistcoat where the watch was ripped out of his pocket. Look at the middle finger of his left hand and you will see the mark of a ring.'

Holmes, who had no doubt already observed all this, nodded. 'Well, Lestrade, I can only say that I know of no thief who would mutilate his victims in such a way.'

'Then, Holmes, I thank you for your assistance. I shall have my driver return you to the comfort of your lodgings.'

The suddenness of this announcement seemed to startle Holmes, but before he could respond, a voice from the woods called out for Lestrade, and a young policeman emerged from the trees. He looked pale and cold and his nose was red.

'What is it, Chaplin?' said Lestrade.

'Thought you ought to know, sir. There's someone else who heard the noises.'

Lestrade looked irritated. 'Never mind the noises. Have you found anything concrete?'

'Not yet, sir.'

'Then get out there and look.'

'Yes, sir.'

But before the young policeman could turn, Holmes said, 'Just a minute. What noises were these, Inspector?'

Lestrade appeared exasperated. 'Holmes, I warned you as we drove here that there were superficial aspects to this case. There is nothing to be gained from paying any attention to them.'

'But you will, at least, permit me to satisfy my curiosity?'

'Tell him, Chaplin,' said the Inspector with a quiet sigh of resignation.

The young policeman brightened. 'Well, sir, there's a story about these woods. . . .'

'Never mind the story,' said the Inspector, 'just repeat what was reported to you.'

'Yes, Inspector. Well, sir, at about two o'clock this morning, someone came to the police station in the village to say there were noises in the wood. Roarings and screamings was how they were described to me. Which is just what they always say.'

'Who?' said my friend.

'Well, we've been getting reports of noises in the woods since about last October. Usually we don't take much notice. This time we did, because they talked about there being human screams as well. Locals think there's something unnatural lives here.'

'You will understand,' said Lestrade witheringly, 'why I prefer not to be waylaid by such nonsense.'

'Nevertheless,' said Holmes, 'if there were indeed noises, that might be significant.'

'I have no doubt there were noises,' replied Lestrade. 'A thief challenges a poor fellow who refuses to give up his money and treasures. The fellow calls for help, the thief roars at him to be silent, the fellow yells even louder, the thief sets about him and the fellow's cries become screams of agony and despair. Such noises would be terrible enough, I think, to give the impression that there was something unnatural on the loose here last night. Well I am certain there was not, unless you deem unnatural the commonplace wickedness of a professional bandit.'

'And yet,' said Holmes, 'it can hardly be considered a mark of the professional to create such a hullaballoo as to wake half the neighbourhood. Are not these fellows traditionally known as "footpads"? And does not that term imply a degree of stealth and a certain subtlety of execution?'

'What are you saying, Holmes?' Lestrade was losing the last vestiges of his patience. 'That you agree with Chaplin and the neighbourhood prattlers? That it was some Unspeakable Thing which did for this man? Old Clootie? Horntoes? Jack Blackheart? The Boglewump?'

'Round here,' put in Chaplin unhelpfully, 'they just call it The Horror.'

'Round here, Chaplin,' said Lestrade, 'They are obviously superstitious bumpkins. Now, Mr Holmes, we must proceed with our search of the woods. The four-wheeler is where we left it and will deliver you direct to your doorstep. Thank you for coming out so early. I am most grateful.'

The Inspector then led young Chaplin away into the trees.

'Well, Doctor,' said my friend, 'it looks as if we have a few moments alone with the body. What do you make of it?'

'It would have taken formidable strength to wrench a man's arm half-off in that fashion,' I said, 'and that blow to the face must have been colossal. This thief is a monstrously powerful fellow.'

'Except that I am almost certain he is no thief.'

'Lestrade seemed determined otherwise.'

'Too determined, Watson. Lestrade is holding something back from us.'

'Well, perhaps we should leave him to it, then.'

'I'm not sure that we can afford to. He will get nowhere if he continues along his current track. And suppose, while he is floundering about, the killer should strike again?'

'We have no reason to think he will, have we, Holmes?'

He looked at me. 'No. You are quite right. No reason. And reason is ninety-nine per cent of the investigator's toolbox.

But you heard what young Chaplin said. Noises have been heard here before. Prattling the neighbours may be, but that does not necessarily make them wrong. However, we need not be wholly dependent upon hearsay. Look at this unfortunate fellow's hands, Watson. They tell a story.'

'They do?'

'Indeed. What do you see?' said my friend.

'Well, the fingertips of the left one are calloused. And there is a fresh scar at the root of the thumb. A bite-mark perhaps. The right hand has fresh blisters. Interestingly, they seem to be a sort of mirror of the callouses on the left hand, around the pads of the fingertips.'

'Excellent. Go on.'

'Some red and black staining on the cuff of the jacket. Ink, I expect, or paint. I think that's about it.'

'It is enough.'

I looked at Holmes in astonishment. 'Enough?'

'To identify him. We know quite a good deal about him now. That he was a ledger-clerk, that he was ambidextrous and that he was an amateur fiddle player who had recently resumed playing after a break of some weeks. That is not bad for a beginning.'

'You deduced all that from the fellow's hand?'

'Oh that was not so difficult. What baffles me is the overcoat. Look. Do you see? There are all these crude rends and tears, and then, just here, a small triangular section of the lining has been carefully snipped out. Curious.'

'I wonder if Lestrade noticed it.'

'I doubt it would have registered with him. Let Lestrade go looking for his monstrous footpad. We shall proceed in quite another direction. But the first stop on our itinerary will be Baker Street and a good breakfast.'

During our journey home, the sun rose upon the frosty streets of the metropolis and a beautiful, crisp, winter morning. After we had eaten a hearty meal, Holmes sent for the page boy and handed him a slip of paper to take to the offices of the evening papers. The advertisement read:

*IF YOU KNOW A LEDGER-CLERK WHO IS AN
AMBIDEXTER, AN AMATEUR FIDDLE-PLAYER, AND WHO
HAS BEEN MISSING FROM HOME SINCE YESTERDAY OR
WHO FAILED TO TURN UP AT HIS PLACE OF WORK
TODAY, CONTACT 221b BAKER STREET, WHERE YOU WILL
BE REWARDED FOR YOUR TROUBLE*

'And now,' I said to Holmes, 'I hope you mean to tell me how you arrived at this description, merely from an examination of that fellow's hands.'

'Well,' said he, 'as always, my friend, it is pitifully straight-forward. You will find the mystery evaporates disappointingly when the light of reason falls upon it.

'Let's begin with the easiest part. Those callouses upon the left fingertips. Now look at my own hand. You see? Callouses in exactly the same places. It was a violinist's hand! Yet there were also those fresh blisters on the right hand, as you noted, almost mirror-images. Well, then, he had swopped hands, and instead of fretting the instrument with his left, was now bowing with his left and fretting with his right. Why? Because of that scar by the thumb. The injury, when fresh, must have stopped him playing for a while, and because he resumed with it only part-healed, he found it easier to change hands.'

'Yet that does not prove he was ambidextrous. Not if he changed over from necessity.'

'Ah. But he *wrote* with his left hand.'

'Did he?'

'Certainly. Remember those ink-stains on the cuff? When a right-handed person writes, his writing trails behind the moving hand, whereas a left-handed person moves his arm to follow the writing. If the ink is wet, his cuff may well mop up some ink as it follows in the furrow of the pen. Now if the fellow wrote with his left hand, yet normally played the fiddle with his right, he was ambidextrous by definition.'

'And a ledger-clerk?'

'Red and black ink, Watson. The red and black stains being about the same size suggested that he used those inks in roughly equal quantities, as people do who are compiling budgets and accounts – black for credit, red for debit. The quantity of the staining, and the fact that it was upon the cuff of such a suit as a clerk might wear to work, suggested strongly that this man was a professional, and not merely a domestic accountant.'

Later that same evening our newspaper advertisement received a reply. 'Dear Sir, I know your man,' was all it said, except that it included a name and address. That the address was in Charlton Village was all the encouragement Holmes needed to order us a cab immediately. We drove down to Lambeth Bridge then through Southwark, taking the Lower Road through Greenwich and from there to Charlton Village. By this time a frost was falling and it was very cold again.

The respondent to our advertisement was Martin Sharpless, a youngish man who had inherited from his family a large and pleasant house in Church Lane. Although not expecting to see us that evening, he showed no signs of surprise upon opening the door to us and being told who we were. In fact, he expressed a particular delight in meeting Holmes and myself, whom he claimed to have heard much about.

'Actually, I am a little of a detective myself. Not in an international sort of way, Mr Holmes, as you are. But I have followed many of your cases, and have even on occasions been able to assist friends with small problems which required a rational analysis.'

'Then we shall get on well,' said Holmes generously. 'Now, what of our ledger-clerk?'

'Yes. I dare say you would like to know who he is,' said Sharpless. 'Well his name is Joseph Beard, he is thirty-five years old, unmarried, and lives here.'

'In this house?' I said, amazed.

'I rent him a small suite of rooms in the basement.'

'Mr Sharpless,' said Holmes gravely, 'would you describe Mr Beard to me, in as much detail as you can.'

'I can do better than that, Mr Holmes. He has a photograph of himself with his mother and sister upon his chest of drawers downstairs.'

The lodger's basement rooms were a far cry from the glory

of the rest of the Sharpless house – small, cramped and untidy, they smelled strongly of damp and the furniture was poor and old. The photograph on the chest of drawers confirmed beyond much doubt that the body discovered in Hanging Wood that morning belonged to Joseph Beard. A young man stood between two women, one arm around the shoulder of the older one, the other around the younger's waist. Despite the terrible disfigurement inflicted by his killer, his picture showed the same uneven hairline and pointed chin and, indeed, the very same suit which we had seen torn and shredded upon the corpse.

'When did you last see your lodger, Mr Sharpless?' asked Holmes.

'Yesterday evening. He is employed at the Loan and Discount Company. He came home from work at the usual time, about six-thirty, and remained here in his rooms until about eleven-thirty.'

'You are sure of that?'

'Positive. He played that confounded fiddle for most of the evening. A habit which, I'm afraid, I find rather tiresome. I have to confess that when the accident stopped him playing just before Christmas I was more than a little relieved.'

'Ah yes,' said Holmes, 'the hand injury. Do you know how he came by it? It looked, I thought, like a bite mark.'

'Ah – then I see you know my lodger better than I. I never saw the wound. If it was a bite, it was not from any animal he kept here. All I know is, that bandage prevented his playing for a few blissful weeks.'

The violin in question lay discarded upon a ragged armchair, along with a bow which had seen better days. Holmes picked it up, weighed it in his hands, and put it down again. 'I must tell you,' he said to Sharpless, 'that Joseph Beard is dead. He was murdered early this morning, some time after midnight, in Hanging Wood.'

'Murdered!'

Sharpless was palpably shocked, doubly so when he heard the terrible details. But he could shed little light upon the habits of his former guest.

'He would go to his job and return, play his fiddle, go out for the evening to a public house and then come home and retire. He never stayed out overnight and was always back before midnight. Which was why, when I saw your advertisement, I felt sure it must be him you were looking for.'

With Sharpless' consent we began a thorough search of Joseph Beard's few possessions. He had indeed, according to Sharpless, had a pocket watch, as Lestrade had surmized, and he had also worn a ring on his right hand. But there was nothing of value in the drawers and cupboards of his rooms, just a few letters from his mother in Ironbridge, a set of draughts and a board, some small ivory figurines and one single book, *ex libris*. It was marked, 'Agnew's Penny Library, Charlton,' and was called *Beak and Talon*.

Upon opening the book, I found it to be a discourse upon cockfighting. There were a few photographs and many drawings of fighting birds in full battle regalia, crested and spurred. I dipped at random into one paragraph.

'It is possible, though a slow process, to harden the beak with the glycerine solution (described at the end of this chapter). The cock's beak, when hard, can be sharpened to a point using a razor or trimming-knife, making it a formidable weapon in combat.'

'Do you know whether Joseph Beard was given to attending such entertainments?' asked Holmes.

'It's possible,' said Sharpless. 'I see the way your mind is working, Mr Holmes. Cockfights, dogfights and the like. You're thinking that's how he might have acquired that wound on his hand.'

'Precisely, Mr Sharpless.'

'I wonder,' Sharpless continued, bolstered by Holmes' approving remark, 'if you think there is any connection between the death of Joseph Beard and that other business in Hanging Wood last year?'

'Last year?'

'You did not hear of it? Of course, it never made the papers.

It was late October. I was taking an early morning walk through the wood and found a large section roped off. There were policemen, and the impression I got was that they were cleaning up after some rather gruesome felony.'

Holmes was furious. 'Watson, it is as I suspected. Lestrade has been hiding something from us. Why was he so determined that this was a case of highway robbery? Because it is more convenient for him to believe in a homicidal thief than in some monster with an appetite for human blood.'

'And yet,' said I, 'since it is, as you say, extraordinary that a thief should trumpet his deeds with growlings and allow his victims the liberty to scream blue murder, the monster becomes the most likely possibility. But what sort of monster could it be?'

'I don't know,' said Holmes, 'and I shall not find out if Lestrade insists on witholding essential information from me. I want you to go to see him, Watson. Afraid of publicity is he? He would be. Monsters in the woods have the effect of making the police appear somewhat lead-footed. Well, then, make it clear that unless he tells us everything he can about this business, he will find himself with more publicity than Mr Barnum's Travelling Circus.

'In the meantime, Mr Sharpless, I would be grateful if you would consent to applying your investigative powers to an important task.'

'Certainly, Mr Holmes. I should feel privileged to help.'

'I should like you to use your knowledge of the neighbourhood to find out whether any bloodsports – dogfights, cockfights, and the like – are conducted here, and if so whether anyone involved in them recognizes Mr Joseph Beard from this photograph.'

'I shall start first thing tomorrow,' said Sharpless, 'and report the results to you.'

'Thank you. And now it is getting late. Doctor Watson and I must be on our way.'

We took a cab together as far as Waterloo Bridge. From there, Holmes went on to Baker Street where he assured me he had to conduct some essential research, while I walked to Scotland Yard in the hope of finding Lestrade still in his office.

It was after midnight when I returned to Baker Street, by which time I had both accomplished my mission and been thoroughly humiliated.

'Watson,' said Holmes as I slumped down in an armed chair, 'was our friend the Inspector helpful?'

'The man's an oaf,' I said, 'besides which, the stove in his office was not lit and I was not favoured with so much as a cup of tea. I trust you have had a pleasant evening?'

'It was necessary,' he said, 'for me to read this book on cockfighting which you found among Joseph Beard's possessions, and to that task I applied myself. But tell me, did you get the information I asked for?'

'I did,' said I, 'but I fear it will be useless to us now.'

'Watson, what can you mean?'

'Things started off well enough. I told him that we had learned that there had been at least one previous murder in Hanging Wood. I did not say how I knew about it. I think he presumed it had been from one of your other police sources. He agreed, at last, to tell me a little about it, and very interesting it turned out to be.

'The victim in that case had been identified as Jasper Adams, a gamekeeper on a local estate. There had been a terrible battering of the body and rending of the garments, just as in the case of Joseph Beard. I persuaded Lestrade to let me see those of the dead man's possessions that had been found upon his person and retained for forensic purposes. This was the most extraordinary part. There was an overcoat, just like Beard's, with a neat triangle of cloth snipped out of the lining.'

'Well, now. Anything else?'

'One small thing. In his pocket they had found a piece of card declaring that the carrier was a member of Agnew's Penny Library – the same library to which Joseph Beard belonged. Not a great coincidence, when one considers they lived in the same neighbourhood, but interesting.'

'Doctor, you have done well. Why so despondent?'

'Because, Holmes, as I say, it is all useless now. Lestrade has made an arrest.'

'What?'

'They brought the fellow in while I was there. Harry Bannister. Lestrade had done what he said he would – followed up those with records of highway robbery not currently in prison. Bannister's had dealings with the police since he was six, lives alone in Charlton and has no alibi for yesterday night. What's more, he apparently keeps a horde of weapons in his shake-down – cudgels, knives, crowbars and the like. Lestrade was jubilant. "Tell Mr Holmes," he said, "that this is one of those cases which exemplifies the triumph of routine procedures over fantastic speculation as a proper method of enquiry." I presume, Holmes, that we will now drop the business,and I for one will not be sorry.'

'Drop it? On the contrary, Watson, we must accelerate our investigations. It is more than likely that Lestrade has arrested an innocent man. First thing tomorrow we shall return to Charlton to visit this penny library. In the meantime, I suggest you retire. I shall stay up. There are some matters to which I wish to give some thought.'

The next morning we travelled back to Charlton as planned, where we found Agnew's Penny Library housed in a rather pleasant lodge in Victoria Road. The building was a domestic residence of which the downstairs part had been given over entirely to the display of books and documents. There were a few small tables for reading and study, at which two or three people were sitting, and a separate office with glass panelling from which the librarian could keep an eye on the movements of her clients.

She was a small, bright-eyed woman of about forty-five or fifty, her grey hair shaped with immaculate precision into a bun, her black dress trimmed with sugar-white lace. She wore, as it seems to me schoolteachers and librarians generally do, regardless of the state of their eyesight, round wire spectacles attached to her neck by a length of ribbon, so that she could, when she chose, let them dangle down upon her chest.

While Holmes browsed through the papers and magazines which were kept in an anteroom near the door, giving him the opportunity to make a cursory inspection of the building, it was left to me to approach the small lady in the glassed cubicle, who was, as I had surmized, Miss Agnew herself, owner and manageress of the penny library. Having instructed me firmly of the necessity to speak, if at all, only in a whisper, so that those reading and studying would not be disturbed, she informed me that members paid one penny per week for each book they borrowed, up to a maximum of five books a week for established members, and that membership entailed the filling in of a form and the payment of a refundable deposit of seven shillings. My exclamation upon receiving this last piece of information met with a firm response.

'If you think that seven shillings is a lot of money, Doctor, you must know very little about the price of books. Many of these have been in my family for generations and are quite irreplaceable. The deposit is a guarantee against theft. Now, would you like to join or not?'

I asked whether it would be possible to look around the library before making a decision, and was told that it would, on condition that we leave our overcoats with Miss Agnew in the glass-panelled cubicle. Books had all too often been smuggled out in the pockets of large garments. Holmes and I complied with Miss Agnew's request and began to wander together about the shelves. The bespectacled, owl-like eyes of the librarian kept careful watch upon us.

Having walked all the shelves and completed his initial survey, Holmes stopped by a particular section. 'While we are here,' he said, 'we may as well see what they have on animal combat. Look – here's one on dogfighting.'

He pulled from the shelves a brown leather-spined volume and opened it at random. An engraving showed a make-shift area of upturned benches from which a baying audience of men, some poor, others evidently wealthier, with waving arms and with faces contorted into pictures of savage ecstasy, were looking down upon the aftermath of a stand-off between two dogs. The beasts were bloody and torn, one still standing, but the other dead or dying, a pool of dark liquid oozing from its mouth. The caption read, *Jack Spot, 1872 Hackney Champion, stands over the crippled body of two-year-old Ripper, who died three days later.*'

'What apalling savagery,' said my friend.

'It is sport to some,' I said.

'Not to the dogs, I'll wager,' he replied. He was about to close the book and return it to the shelf when he said, in slightly quieter tones, 'Miss Agnew, the librarian, is looking at us again. I dare say she thinks I am going to pocket the book. There. I shall replace it.'

'She has turned away now,' I said. 'She seems to be busy again at her desk.'

'Then let us collect our coats and return to Baker Street. I feel we should have learned something here, Watson, but if we have, I am not sure yet what it is. Now, which of us is to have the pleasure of explaining to Miss Agnew that we do not wish to pay seven shillings to join her library?'

We caught a train back into London and, having taken luncheon at Oates' in the Strand, continued on to Baker Street by cab. Holmes and I sat opposite one another during the journey and, at one point, he leaned across to me with an apology and pulled a couple of hairs from my overcoat, one from the lapel, the other from the sleeve.

'Now, where did you pick these up, Watson?' He stretched one of them out between his hands and looked at it closely. 'They are certainly not yours, either by length or colour. And they are very coarse indeed.'

'Oates' restaurant, I dare say,' I replied.

'It is possible, except that I noticed one of a very similar colour and length upon the dress of Miss Agnew at the library.'

'Well, then, it was there.'

He nodded but said nothing. From his expression I knew that something had set off a train of thought of too great a momentum to be deflected by anything I might say. We rode on another mile and were just coming into Cavendish Square when he said suddenly, 'Yes, Pfeiffer is the man.'

'I beg your pardon, Holmes?'

'I'm sorry, Watson, I was thinking aloud. Dr Otto Pfeiffer is an old acquaintance of mine. He is currently at the Zoological Institute and I think he may be able to help us with this business. But first we'll smoke a cigar and chew the matter over a little. He lectures in the daytime and I want to be certain to catch him.'

Back in our rooms, with pipes lit, we sat opposite one another before the fire. Holmes poured us a brandy.

'Now, my friend,' he said, 'we have been two days upon this case. We have seen the body, identified the corpse, discovered where the victim lived, visited his landlord and his librarian and ascertained that there was at least one previous victim of a similar crime in the same place only a few months ago. Inspector Lestrade, with only a fraction of that information, has succeeded in arresting a man. What are we to conclude? That he is more competent than we are? Could Lestrade be right and Harry Bannister guilty?'

An answer was clearly expected and I endeavoured, knowing how much imprecision of thought irritated my friend, to decorate my somewhat negative speculations with the sort of gloss I thought would be to his taste.

'Well frankly, I do not see how it fits together, Holmes. Two men on occasions several months apart, are hideously murdered in Hanging Wood by some assailant or assailants unknown. They do not, according to Lestrade's files, appear to have been acquainted with one another, they mixed in different circles and they had only these three things in common: first, both were residents of Charlton, second, both were members of Miss Agnew's Penny Library and third, both wore topcoats with a triangle of cloth cut out of the lining. I confess I am spectacularly and comprehensively baffled.'

'Thank you, Watson. That was a thorough-going and accurate appraisal. But you allow yourself to be dismayed by the seemingly disparate nature of the facts. Remember that tripartite *sine qua non* for any murder: a killer, a victim and a motive. We have identified the victim, and would be helped enormously if we were able to lay our finger upon the motive. Now, Lestrade maintains that Joseph Beard was casually killed in the course of a robbery, but we have dismissed the notion of a casual killing because of the extraordinary and terrible nature of the execution. What our friend the Inspector refuses to acknowledge is the real motive – for is it not altogether apparent that this was a *crime passionel* of some kind? Does it not strike you that the prevailing emotion of our murderer was one of absolute and uncontrolled *fury*?'

'Yes,' said I, 'it does.'

'Yet the fellow's pocketwatch and ring *were* taken. Is a hot-blooded killer given to such petty venality?'

'I suppose not.'

'Why then would he steal them? Because they bore the victim's name or initials, and therefore might have lead to the killer. In which case, we are indeed on the right track.'

'Excellent,' I said, 'but where does that leave us?'

'It leaves us, said Holmes, with a sigh, 'at a point where we need more data. I am off to see Pfeiffer at the Zoological Institute. I shall be as quick as I can but the investigations may take some time, and besides, dear old Otto will no doubt want to talk. Expect me late.'

Within a few moments he had collected his hat and coat and was gone.

It was early evening and dark before I heard the street door open and shut again. I had spent the afternoon writing a letter to an old friend and tidying up some papers and I was rather looking forward to Holmes' company, and to finding out what he had discovered from Professor Pfeiffer at the Institute. However, it was Mrs Hudson, not Holmes, who opened the sitting-room door.

'A Mr Sharpless is here to see you, Doctor. He said you would want to see him. Something to do with the case you and Mr Holmes are working on.'

'Oh! Why, yes. Please show him in.'

Sharpless was very disappointed to discover that Holmes was not in. He had come all the way from Charlton specifically to report upon his investigations of that morning, which he had evidently executed with immense energy and determination.

'Perhaps you'd be prepared to confide the details to me,' I

said, 'for I cannot say what time my colleague will be back.'

'Yes, Doctor, of course. I know that you and Mr Holmes work closely together. Well, you remember that he had asked me to make enquiries about blood sports? I decided that my acquaintances in local public houses would know whatever there was to be known, so I mounted up and rode around my favourites – the Rose of Denmark, the White Horse, the Roupell, the Antigallican, the Horse and Groom, and found out nothing at all until I got to the Lads of the Village in Manor Way. I won't say the name of the man I talked to, as he asked me to keep it confidential. He told me yes, there had been some dog-fighting in the village now and again, but never in Hanging Wood. He said the wood was never the sort of place for it, as the sound carried too far. These things would always be conducted in a cellar in a public house, or down at the wharves away from anywhere. When I asked him about Joseph Beard he said, "Jo Beard? Yes, he used to come some times. Till he got bitten just before Christmas by Toby Hocking's wild little pug. He's never been back since." He said there were no other sports going on in the neighbourhood. He would know if there were. He was adamant about that. Well, that was interesting, but I felt I wanted to know more about this animal-fighting business. Mr Holmes, of course, had taken Beard's book on cockfighting with him, so I thought, "I shall go and join Miss Agnew's penny library. I may learn something, besides, from retracing Beard's footsteps." Well, I did just that. I roamed the shelves and in the end chose this. *Gainsborough's Guide to Fighting Dogs*. It is not very pleasant.'

'I believe I can imagine the drift of it,' I said.

'Yes,' he said, riffling through the book, 'some very unpleasant pictures...' but here Sharpless suddenly stopped. Something between the pages of the book had caught his eye. It looked like a bookmark or a yellow slip of paper and I watched as he read whatever was written or imprinted upon it. Then he shut the book quickly and said, 'Doctor Watson, what is he time?'

'Eight-thirty.'

'I must return to Charlton immediately. Forgive me.'

'But what is it?' I asked.

'I cannot say. It is all most confusing. I must get home and collect a lantern and make an assignation by eleven. Call upon me tomorrow and I shall tell you everything but, by your leave, I must go now.'

Half an hour after the street door slammed shut, I heard it once again open and close and Holmes strode up the stairs and entered the sittingroom.

'Watson,' he said, 'I have had a most interesting and rewarding evening.'

'And I too,' I said. 'Young Sharpless has been here. He is a precipitous fellow to be sure. He travelled all the way here to report the results of his investigations to you, and finding you gone, was in the course of reporting to me instead, when he suddenly shot up and said he must return to Charlton for an assignation.'

'Did he say where?'

'No. Only that he would need a lantern for it.'

'A lantern! But what made him recollect his appointment so suddenly?'

'I'm not sure that he did recollect it. He seemed to have found something in the book he was carrying.'

I explained to Holmes about Sharpless' enquiries at the local public houses, and how he had gone on a visit to the library. To my amazement this seemed to trouble Holmes intensely.

'The library!'

'Yes, I supposed he had much the same idea as we did, that it would be useful to. . .'

'Watson – our overcoats, quickly!'

'Oh. We are going out?'

'Very likely, but for now, I simply wish to look at them.'

When I had brought the coats he flung them on the floor, opened them at the front and examined them swiftly.

'There!'

From the lining of each coat, a small triangle of cloth had been neatly snipped away.

'But who would have done that?' I said.

'Only one person could have done it. Miss Agnew.'

'While we were in the library, of course, when she had the coats in her office. But what on earth for?'

Holmes, with a grave air, began to put on his coat. 'A dreadful thought has occurred to me, Watson. If we are to save young Sharpless from a terrible fate, we must get to Charlton as fast as two men ever travelled.' He went to his room, emerging two minutes later to marshall me downstairs.

He was silent, however, as the cab thundered through the darkened London streets and this, I knew, was because he considered his speculations to be incomplete, and would hazard no mere opinion. But, some good while later, as we rode along the rough lane that took us into Hanging Wood, he said, 'I have let this business make a fool of me, Watson. Let us hope it will not make a corpse of Mr Martin Sharpless.'

The cabby being unwilling to wait for us in such a shadowy place, Holmes paid him off, apparently giving no thought as to how we were to get home from this remote spot so late at night. The moon was not due for some hours, and though it was a clear, starry night, the woodland seemed almost pitch black. It was chilling to remember that a man had been found dead there only the previous morning, and the stories of the Horror in the wood, which Lestrade had dismissed cavalierly, no longer seemed quite so implausible. The forest, in the darkness, was a cold and primitive place. Men did not seem welcome there.

We lit the lanterns we had brought with us.

'You haven't told me,' I said, 'what it is we are looking for.'

'For Sharpless,' Holmes replied.

'Here in the forest?'

'Yes.'

'You think he is dead?'

'I hope not.'

'Do you know why he came here, then?'

'Perhaps.'

'Then what do you expect to find?'

'I have no clear expectations. We will simply explore the woods until we discover something.'

We had already walked into the wood a good way from the

track. The wind, light but bitterly cold, shook the trunks of the sparser trees. It was a desolate place. There seemed to be nothing living among the wintered branches. Suddenly Holmes stopped walking to listen, and it was then that I heard the first sound, a low, strangulated growl, very deep, which, like the murmuring of a volcano, seemed to issue from the depths of some elemental anger.

'Here,' said Holmes. Reaching into his pocket, he handed me a pistol.

'But you?'

'I have one too.'

Then we heard other sounds, first, a high-pitched wail, much more like the cry of a man, then, somewhere in the darkness, running footsteps.

'Mr Sharpless,' Holmes yelled, 'It's Sherlock Holmes.'

The only reply was another distant growl. Again Holmes called. He signalled me to join him and we shouted and shouted until we had worn the edges off our voices. At last, a voice called back, far off and utterly desperate, 'Mr Holmes! For pity's sake.'

'Over here!' Holmes yelled to the man in the darkness, 'Over here!' and we ran pell mell in the direction of the voice.

Running in a forest at night is not easy. Twice I fell, leaving Holmes sprinting on ahead of me, seeming to find his way by some sort of nocturnal instinct. Suddenly there was a terrible scream. The growling changed in pitch, becoming closer and more threatening. I had completely lost sight of Holmes now, and staggered along in his wake guided only by the twinkling light of his lantern. Then there was a pistol shot and everything was quiet. Fear of what I might find ahead slowed my progress, but I dragged myself towards Holmes' light, which now seemed to have stopped moving and to hang still among the dark twists of trees ahead. I came at last to a clearing, and what I saw there almost caused me to drop my lantern.

The monster was lurking in the shadows twenty feet from where my friend stood with his pistol raised. Next to Holmes' feet, huddled in a whimpering ball, was Sharpless. The monster's eyes reflected Holmes' lantern in two amber flames. Its growl was now low and deep, like that of a dog at bay. But this was no dog. It was eight feet tall and stood upright as broad as a church door. Holmes fired his pistol, not at the creature, but just above its head. Shattered pieces of beechwood flew this way and that as the shot echoed about the forest.

'What is it?' I whispered.

'A bear,' said Holmes. 'According to Professor Pfeiffer, a Canadian grisly bear.'

'Good Lord. Why don't you shoot it?'

'No, Watson, I will not do that. There is something even deadlier we must wait for.'

As we waited, that great shadow lurked threateningly close, neither advancing nor retreating, the reflected fires blazing in its eyes, for perhaps three or four minutes. Sharpless stopped whimpering and turned his head toward the trees. Twigs snapped in the forest, then there came the clumsy approach of running footsteps, then the flicker of a lantern, and at last there emerged into the clearing the small and somewhat bedraggled figure of Miss Agnew, proprietress of the penny library. She stopped directly she saw Holmes and stood frozen for a moment assessing the situation. She shouted, 'Don't shoot that animal! He doesn't know what he's doing.'

Holmes replied softly, keeping his gun levelled at the creature, 'Indeed, Miss Agnew. No one can blame a bear for being wild. Especially one which has been excited into a frenzy. The true savage is the human being who will put an animal up to such a bloody business.'

'So you say,' replied the woman with surprising ferocity, 'and what about the bloody business done by those who set poor dumb creatures to fight one another to death. What about Dodger? There was never a dearer creature than that pup. Why don't you point your gun at the villain that stole him from his kennel one night and put him to fight. Or at the lovely gentlemen baying and screaming like wolves while they watched the dear little soul's throat be torn out.'

'I have no more love for such men than you do,' said Holmes, 'but to set a wild beast upon a man is murder, whatever the reasons for it. Now, if you wish to save this creature's life, I suggest that you shackle it immediately. Then we shall get it to its cage. And you, Miss Agnew, I fear to yours.'

And indeed, within the hour, the bear lay sleeping in its cage in the converted summerhouse behind the lodge where Miss Agnew housed her penny library, while its owner was installed behind another set of bars in a cell at the police station.

Later, Holmes and I sat around a fire in Sharpless' house. He had recovered sufficiently to prepare us some soup, for that hour in Hanging Wood had chilled us all to the bone. While we ate, Holmes explained the entire business to us.

'Miss Agnew's vendetta was against anyone who attended those so-called sporting occasions where animals are provoked to fight – dogfights, cockfights, bear-baitings. But such events are usually held in secret. How was she, a rather prim, middle-aged woman, to gain access to those who attended them? Well, she began to assemble in her library a stock of books dealing with those very sports she detested. Whenever a reader requested such a book, she would insert into it, as it was issued, an invitation to attend some fictional spectacle of animal combat that very night.'

'That piece of paper I found in the book, Doctor Watson,' said Sharpless, 'which made me up and leave you so hastily, was an invitation to attend what it referred to as "sensational animal sport in Hanging Wood." That was what confused me. My informant had assured me the wood was never used for such diversions – so what could this mean? I attended, thinking I might discover something. I had hardly been here ten minutes before I heard that creature. I cannot tell you what agonies of terror I went through in that moment when I realized that I was to be its quarry.'

'But what was the significance,' I asked, 'of those triangles of cloth cut from the linings of coats?'

'Like any hunting beast,' said Holmes, 'a bear has a phenomenal sense of smell. But it also has a good memory. My colleague Professor Pfeiffer explained how it would be possible to arouse such a creature to anger by reminding it of past cruelties. If you noticed the scars on the animal's back and legs you might have surmised, as I did, that Miss Agnew had rescued him at some time from a life of torment. Now, by introducing him to the scent of a man on those triangles of cloth, Miss Agnew could entice him to associate a particular chosen quarry with his old hatred, arousing him to a vengeful fury.'

'But surely she didn't mutilate the lining of all of her clients' coats,' I said.

'She did not need to. Only those who showed an interest in books in the blood-sports section were possible targets. It was when she saw us pick up that book, Watson, that our coats were doctored. But we did not take the next step of borrowing it. Had we done so, we would have found a note inside like the one Mr Sharpless found. Even then, we would only have been in danger had we accepted the invitation to Hanging Wood. It was an ingenious method designed to earmark only those who would actually attend blood-sport meetings.'

'There must have been times, though,' I said, 'when the invitation was not taken up and she and her bear waited in vain in the woods for victims.'

'Certainly. Hence those local rumours of the growling Horror, when the creature got restless.'

'But to go out like that,' said Sharpless, 'cold-bloodedly looking for people to kill . . . it's so dreadful.'

'Indeed,' said Holmes, 'but that a person's only friend in the world should be a dumb animal – that, perhaps, is a little dreadful too.'

Within a year Miss Felicity Agnew had kept her appointment with justice and I believe the bear was trundled off to some zoo to live out its days, leaving Hanging Wood a quieter place though, naturally enough, legends being legends, they speak even today in Charlton village of the Old Horror. Mr Sharpless, however, who wrote to me a few years after the incident, by that time a married man and a father, told me he had come to think of the wood as a very sweet and agreeable place, where pigeons cooed and bluebells flowered and children played gaily, fearless of anything more sinister than a grey squirrel or a fat bumblebee.